The Education of Mattie Dobson

Maggie Redding

For Diana Evans,
a Grammar School Girl,
with love

FIRST FORM
1950-1951

CHAPTER ONE

No one expected Mattie Dobson to get a place at the Grammar School, least of all Mattie herself because she knew what a pig's ear she had made of the interview. All the other pupils attending for an interview were with a parent. Mattie had come alone. Even before the start, she felt she was all wrong.

"Tell me," one of the interviewers asked her, "what do you like doing in your spare time?" They were sitting behind a huge desk. That alone made her feel small and silly.

She took a deep breath. "I like thinking," she said. "I sit and think poems. Then I write them down. Then I think about pictures for them and I draw them."

"What are the poems and pictures about?"

"Owls, sometimes. Or thunderstorms. And my sister, Libby. She's left home." Mattie lowered her eyes.

"Is that sad?"

Libby had left a ten shilling note for her, under her hairbrush, on the dressing table. "Very sad," she said. They were kind which was such a surprise. But she must not talk about Libby. "And I think about mountains. I would like to live in the mountains." Oh, dear. She was stupid and now they would know she was stupid.

"What would you do if you lived in the mountains?"

"I would keep sheep. I would have a sheep-dog. And I'd watch birds."

"Do you like birds?"

What a daft question. Everyone likes birds. She wished she'd not mentioned them. Or mountains. They had nothing to do with the Grammar School. Some birds were lovely. Some weren't.

"I like some birds. Not starlings. They're noisy. They squabble. Though they have lovely colours. But they are vicious. And gannets. They are – they're single-minded, sort of. I saw some at the seaside once."

The woman smiled. She asked a few more questions then the man, who wrote a lot, also had some questions, one about gannets, then it was time to go.

Mattie almost ran along the gravel path to the gates of the Grammar School. She had made herself look silly. Still, it didn't matter. She didn't have to go to the Grammar School. Thoughts of her best friend, Carol Tillington, calmed her. Carol had no ambitions to go anywhere but Sittendon Secondary Modern School. Mattie strolled the rest of the way home, not bothering to fasten her coat. When the woman had asked her about Libby, she had wanted to cry. It was sad about Libby. Last week she had left home without explanation, without saying goodbye.

"Gone?" Mattie had said when Mum told her. "Gone where?"

"To a new job. In a boarding school."

"To be a teacher?" Mattie had said.

"Don't be silly. Libby's not clever enough to be a teacher. To help the matron look after the girls. She'll be a skivvy."

Mattie was shocked at this. "Without telling me?"

"Yes. Libby can be a bit thoughtless."

"Thoughtless? I think it's unkind. She didn't even say good-bye."

"Yes, well. I don't approve of what she's done."

Libby was eighteen. She had always seemed to Mattie to be clever, thoughtful, responsible even.

"What about her job in the hairdresser's? I thought she liked it."

"Oh, she got tired of it," Mum had said.

"Did she leave an address so I can write to her?"

"She'll be writing soon. She's a silly girl. Don't keep on." And Mum's mouth went into a straight line which meant that was the end of that topic of conversation.

So Mattie had not kept on, not to her mother. But to herself, she had, inside her head, all the time, questions, going round and round with never an answer, all in the space left in her head from the Grammar School which occupied a lot of it. Anyway, she really wanted to go there, to the Grammar School. Since her sister had left home, she had been reading the books that had belonged to her. Over the years, Libby had compiled quite a collection and now Mattie had access to them, all of them. Mostly, they were school stories, the Dimsie books, the Chalet School series, and the Abbey Girl stories. Mattie loved them all. Never, in one million years, would she be able to go to boarding school, like in the books. The Grammar School, however, was the next best thing. She would learn French, and maybe play lacrosse, or more likely, hockey. And the uniform! Mattie dreamed of wearing a gymslip.

* * *

"What was it like, then?"

Mum, white faced, had risen from her sick bed and now sat by the kitchen range where a half-hearted fire smouldered, for it was cold for May.

5

"It was, you know, just talking." Mattie shrugged.

"What did they ask you?" Mum persisted in her questioning. She was hard to divert.

Mattie was not sure if her mother was grim for some reason she did not understand or whether it was because she was ill. Mum's dark hair was greasy, going grey and scraped back off her face. Blue Irish eyes, fringed with black lashes, were hidden under a permanent frown. Life was hard for her mother, Mattie knew.

"Oh, what I liked, books and things. Are you better?"

"Better than I was. Did Dad go to work afterwards?" Dad worked for the Council, in Parks and Gardens, a job he loved but which did not pay well. He had taken time off to accompany Mattie to the gates of the Grammar School, but only that far. He went off to work after that.

"I suppose so. Did you go to the Council Offices today?" Mum made a weekly pilgrimage to the Housing Office in the Town Hall to beg for a council house. She suffered from poor health and Frank, Mattie's brother, was asthmatic. The house, sixty-three, Honeyhill Street, was damp. In the 'front' room wallpaper peeled off the wall, on its own, to reveal black mould. The stairs were a problem for Mum, two flights of them. There was no hot water, no bathroom, only one cold tap in the scullery and an outside toilet.

The boys, Frank, nine, and Tony, seven, came home from school, scrambling in through the scullery door.

"Did you get in?" Frank wanted to know.

"What d'you mean?" Mattie poured tea for her mother and for herself. She glanced up at Frank. He

6

shook his head and moved to the fireguard around the old fashioned range. Socks and the boys' underpants hung there to dry.

"The Grammar. Are you going there?"

"They don't tell you. You have to wait."

"Why aren't you going to St Catherine's? That's where the girls go from our school."

"It's too far," Mattie said.

"You won't get in the Grammar," Tony said. "You have to be clever to go there."

"You have to be clever to go to St Catherine's, don't you?" Frank said.

"If I don't get into the Grammar, I go to the secondary modern," Mattie explained. She sat down at the table.

"You should go to St Catherine's," Frank said. "It's Catholic. And even if you don't pass the scholarship, you could go to the secondary modern stream there."

"The Grammar is close to here," Mum said, popping a pill into her mouth and washing it down with tea. "I saw Carol's mother yesterday. Carol is going to the secondary modern here. She says the Grammar School uniform is expensive. You have to get it from that store, Phillips'. It's too far to go to St Catherine's."

"You get a grant," Mattie said.

"I'll believe that when I see it," Mum said.

Mattie drained her cup and turned away. She crept upstairs to change out of her best jumper and skirt. Her mother's attitude to the Grammar School was upsetting. It had been her father's choice, the Grammar School. He was thrilled that Mattie had passed the written exam and got as far as the interview. He resisted anything the parish priest, Father Tully, suggested. Mum had been ready to accept the secondary modern for Mattie or even the lower stream at St Catherine's, ten miles away in Ammerfield. Dad was set against St Catherine's because it was so far away and was Father Tully's preference.

Mattie reached the bedroom which she had shared with Libby. From the kitchen, a semi-basement, there were two flights of stairs to mount. The house was in a row of Victorian terraced houses. Behind the kitchen was the cellar. This was underground, at the front of the house, with a coal hole for the sacks of coal to be tipped down by the coalman. The cellar smelled of damp and coal. Mattie feared the cellar, associating it with the day, towards the end of the war, when the family had sheltered there as a doodlebug had gone over. Everyone was waiting for the explosion after the distinctive noise of the engine cut out. When it came, it was a hard, shattering bang that had shaken her to the core. She had clutched her heart. The sound had gone right into it. She had been five years old at the time.

The bedroom overlooked a long, narrow garden and fields beyond them. From this side of the house the drop to the backyard was a long way down. She could see the door of the outside toilet.

She scanned Libby's bookshelves as she changed her clothes. Whatever happened, whether she went to the Grammar School or to the secondary modern school, she would not need her present school clothes after July. If she went to the Grammar School she would have a new uniform. If she went to the secondary modern school she would be able to wear what she liked, like now, but have new ones.

She selected an Angela Brazil story from Libby's

collection, before going downstairs, wishing Libby was still at home.

Mattie's heart did a flip as she approached her school the next morning. She was going to have to give an account of her interview yesterday. By the gate, a huge board proclaimed that this was St Angela's RC primary school. Above the words were the Papal crossed keys and a mitre, St Peter's keys. Her feelings about this notice and its size were confused. She was expected to be proud of her school yet there were times when the pupils were tormented by aggressive young people from other schools. She could never understand why Catholics were mocked, even hated. You had to be hated to have stones thrown at you by a stranger.

"How did you get on, Mattie, dear?" Veronica Fitzgerald's mother was standing at the gate, having at that moment delivered Veronica to the school.

"I don't know, Mrs Fitzgerald. It seemed like any other conversation with two grown-ups. But I'm not worried. It's not important, is it?"

"But it's very important, isn't it, Veronica? It's about your future, isn't it?"

Veronica squeezed her face into a superior smile. Mattie had never felt easy about this girl ever since she had been told that Mum used to work for Mrs Fitzgerald. The Fitzgeralds lived in a big, detached house on Gracehill, the most select area of Sittendon.

"What did you do there?" Mattie had asked Mum.

"I cleaned her house. From top to bottom. So I knew everything she had."

"What did she have?"

"Everything. You name it, she had it. And the latest model." Mum was vague about the facts but the feeling was loud and clear. Mattie's imagination would have to fill in what Mum left out.

Mattie's best friend at St Angela's was Carol Tillington. On this morning, as on many mornings, Carol came tumbling into school late, only achieving her mark in the register by a hair's breadth of a second.

"Are you going?" Carol hissed across the classroom to Mattie.

"I don't know yet," Mattie hissed back.

"Carol Tillington, will you please be quiet," Sister Rose called in a stern voice.

"I only…" Carol began.

"Don't only, please, Carol."

Carol was a slender girl with wispy fair hair and a long face. She was the youngest of a family of five children, all of whom had left school now. Mum, when she first met Carol, described her as 'a wan little creature'. Ever since, Mattie had felt she had to look after her friend. Now Carol would have to wait until playtime to find out if Mattie knew if she would be going to the Grammar School. Mattie explained that they had not told her at the interview.

"I'm glad," Carol said, misunderstanding. "I don't want you to leave me. I'm going to the secondary modern."

"They might still choose me," Mattie said, worried about Carol's assumption.

"I'm praying they don't."

"That's not kind."

"It wouldn't be kind if you went to the Grammar School and left me. I'd have no best friend at the secondary modern."

This Mattie did not want to hear. She and Carol had

been best friends for years, since they had first started school.

"Yes, you would. I'd still be your friend. I'd see you evenings and on Saturdays. We can go round the market together, like we did at Whitsun."

Carol was not interested in speculation. Mattie looked at her. She didn't know what to think. Life without Carol would be unimaginable. She and Carol told each other everything. Only recently, Mattie had sat down with her in a dusty corner of the playground to tell her about Libby.

"She's just gone," she had said, tears hovering.

Carol had regarded her with sympathy. "Can't you ask your Mum where she is?"

"I have. She just says she's gone to a boarding school to help look after the girls. She never says where this is, is it far, if I can go and see her, if she will come home for a visit. She changes the subject."

"Can you write to her?" Writing was Carol's worst subject at school, so to raise the suggestion showed she was listening properly.

"How? I don't know her address. Mum says I can put a note in with hers and not to say things to make Libby feel bad about going."

"Sounds fishy to me," Carol had said.

Now, she said to Carol, "You'd have all the others from our class." She still might get into the Grammar School. "All the others who aren't going to St Catherine's."

"No, I wouldn't. Not a best, best friend. Not a best, best friend in school. And anyway, there's not many going to the Secondary Modern. Most are going to St Catherine's, Grammar and Sec."

"Perhaps I won't get in."

That was what Mum said.

The weather became warmer. Mattie came home from school one day to find Mum sitting in the kitchen, the picture of despair.

"What's wrong, Mum?" Mattie said, thinking her mother might be ill.

Mum startled. "Oh, I forgot the time." She had the look about her that caused Mattie to think she had been crying. As Mattie gazed at her, she passed a casual hand over her face.

"Have you seen Veronica today?"

"She wasn't in school."

"I saw Mrs Fitzgerald. Veronica went for an interview this morning. At the Grammar School. She came out crying."

"Veronica did?"

"Mrs Fitzgerald said they were harsh with her, poor Veronica."

"Everything upsets Veronica."

"She said, Mrs Fitzgerald did, that Father Tully doesn't like children in the parish going to the Grammar School."

"I know. But why?"

"Because it's better for them, Mrs Fitzgerald said, and because there are communist teachers at the Grammar School."

Mattie had no idea what a communist teacher was.

"Veronica is applying to St Catherine's. If she doesn't get in there, they'll pay for a private school."

Like in the books. A private school. Lucky old Veronica.

"Can you pay? I mean, do people pay for private

schools just because they can't get into the Grammar?"

"Oh yes, especially when they're thick. Mattie, you've just got to get into that Grammar School."

This was a change, Mum being all for the Grammar School. Mattie put out a calming hand to touch her mother's, but Mum drew hers back.

"I can't do anything about it now, Mum, only hope, can't I?"

"And pray?"

"Pray? So's we feel good about the Fitzgeralds feeling bad?"

Mum laughed. Her teary eyes met Mattie's for the first time.

"Mattie, it's not being poor that bothers me. I can manage that. I cope. I'm used to it. It's being looked down on, that's what I don't like. Like Mrs Fitzgerald does it. It's the lack of respect. I would like people to respect me."

* * *

"If I said I had some good news for you, Martha, what would you be wanting to hear?" Sister Louise, the Head Teacher, had met her in the corridor at school.

Mattie raised her eyes, daring to whisper it. "That I have passed the scholarship?"

"You have indeed passed the Eleven-plus to the Grammar School," Sister Louise smiled. "Well done, Martha. I am proud of you. You have a wonderful future ahead of you. You will be hearing in the post very soon, or at least, your parents will. Let's get this right, though. You don't pass a scholarship. You win a scholarship. You pass an exam to gain it. And nowadays

13

we call it the Eleven-plus, the exam. It's not a scholarship any longer, though I know people talk about it like that."

Mattie left, glowing, despite the correction. So Sister Louise didn't care too much about the communist teachers at the Grammar School. That was all right then. She would tell Carol in the morning because Mum and Dad must be told first and she needed time to think about how to tell Carol.

Mum was delighted to hear the news, of course, then proceeded to worry about paying for the uniform. Mattie could not be bothered to remind her that a grant was available. She would find out in good time.

"How do I get this grant?" Mum kept saying.

"Ask Mattie," Frank said, refusing to be surprised or pleased. "She's the clever one round here."

"Can I write and tell Libby?"

"Of course. Next time I write to her."

"Why can't you give me her address?"

"Libby is busy, Mattie. Don't bother her."

"Libby wouldn't think that was bothering her, if I was telling her about the Grammar School. Anyway, I want to ask her advice."

"About what?"

"About Carol. She's upset about me going to the Grammar."

"You won't want to bother with her once you get there. You should drop her, and the sooner the better."

Mattie was confused. She had a suspicion that such advice was not sound and that Libby would say something else. She went upstairs to her room, to stand at the window gazing over the hazy fields and rows of gardens that stretched from the terraced houses. She perched on her bed and wrote a poem in the notebook Libby had given her for Christmas.

'Libby, I miss you.
Where have you gone
With no good-bye?
Will you be long?'

Underneath she drew a tiny sketch of the trees on the skyline to remind Libby of the view from their bedroom window and gave it to her mother to send to Libby.

* * *

When the letter arrived, informing Mr and Mrs Dobson that their daughter, Martha, had succeeded in gaining a place at Sittendon Grammar School, there were also details about obtaining a grant towards the uniform. Mum said she hoped it would be enough.

The family was told the news. They crowded into the basement kitchen to celebrate that same evening. Aunt Delia, Mum's sister, her five children and Grandma, as well as other aunts and uncles who lived further than Sittendon.

"I can't see any of my lot getting into the Grammar School," Aunt Delia said.

"No," Mattie said, "you'd want the girls to go to St Catherine's. It's nearer to you."

"Or the Christian Brothers," Mattie's brother Frank said.

"You don't want the boys to go there, surely," Mum said. "They beat them there."

"Saves me doing it," Delia laughed. She would rather talk about her own family than her sister's. Mattie's success was a glaring breach of family tradition.

"I'm not going to the Christian Brothers," Frank said.

"You'll do as you are told," Mum said.

Grandma said she would knit a woolly hat and scarf for Mattie.

"What colours?" she said, "to go with the uniform, you know." Grandma would not acknowledge that the Grammar School uniform was anything special.

Mattie regarded her in horror. She had seen the school uniform, she had seen pupils around the town wearing it. Not one had ever had anything out of place, not anything that was not 'regulation school uniform', as it was expressed in the brochure that had come with the offer of a place and the application form for the grant.

"Navy blue," Mattie told Grandma.

"I'll get knitting right away."

The next day, at school, during playtime, she told Carol.

"It's definite," she said.

"What is?" Carol said.

"The Grammar School. I'm going."

Carol said nothing. She looked away. When she turned back, Mattie could see she was crying.

"I'll still be your friend," she said.

"How long for?"

The bell went then, so Mattie did not have time to answer. For the rest of the day, Carol was unusually quiet. Mattie wanted to talk about the Grammar School, but dared not in case Carol really got the huff about it.

As they were about to leave for home at the end of the day, Mattie said to her, "You know, I'm upset because you're upset."

"What about?" Carol said.

"About the Grammar School and me going."

"Oh, forget about that. So long as you come round the market with me on Saturday."

"So nothing's changed?"

" 'Course not!" Carol said with some enthusiasm and Mattie smiled.

* * *

The end of term came, the Leavers' Party took place. On Mattie's mind was the buying of the new school uniform. The outfitters who supplied the Grammar School uniform, a large, old-fashioned department store, Phillips' had the reputation of providing only the best. Mattie was filled with awe on entering the hallowed portals. The assistants were suave men in neat suits with a deferent manner and women, sleek and slender in black dresses with not a hair out of place. Mum was addressed as 'madam' when asking for directions to the department for school uniforms. She had dressed in an attempt to meet these high standards and Mattie knew she had failed to do so. Mum's unease showed.

"I think, Mattie, you should have a size larger gym slip, to allow for growth," Mum said in the voice she put on for doctors, teachers and the people at the Council Housing Office.

"Mum, I'll look like an orphan," Mattie said, wishing Libby was with them and able to advise Mum.

"I'm afraid the young lady is right, madam," the assistant said. "It would be false economy. The gym slip is only worn for the first two years."

"Then what?" Mum said, forgetting her best voice and using her normal one.

"It's a skirt, after that, madam. From the Third Year."

"Oh, I didn't know that." The best voice came back. "There aren't any regulation shoes and socks, though, are there?"

Was Mum was trying to be funny?

"No, but there are regulation navy blue knickers for gym, to go under the 'divided' skirt."

"Divided skirt?"

How the assistant stopped herself laughing, Mattie couldn't imagine.

"For PT, and gym, madam."

The total was added up and Mum was told, in a discreet voice, the amount.

"Oh, is that all?" Mum said loudly and proceeded to flourish the required pound notes.

CHAPTER TWO

The day arrived on which Mattie was to attend the Grammar School for the first time.

Carol had been quiet on their last outing together. Mattie was confused. How could she be made to wish she wasn't going to the Grammar School, when everyone else thought it was a good thing, except Mum sometimes? The grant had been spent wisely. The night before, the uniform was laid out on Libby's bed so that Mattie could gaze on it. She did, with anxiety and excitement mixed. Sleep was difficult. When she dressed in the morning, her blouse was new and stiff. Her gym slip felt stuffy. Her tie choked her. She needed to have lessons from Dad on how to tie it. Her nervous fingers, or her taut brain, caused her to fumble. In the end, Dad did it for her.

Accompanied by Dad, Mattie set off for the Grammar School, Mum smiling proudly from the front doorway. This was an occasion on which Mum could hold her head high. So far, there had been no word from Libby, not even to congratulate her or to wish her luck.

The Grammar School was a good fifteen minutes' walk away. Mattie and her Dad arrived at the school gates as other pupils were milling around in a dense mass. Some of them were big, almost adults. She needed to sigh, to catch her breath. She knew exactly what she had to do but she was still nervous. Written instructions had been posted to her parents. She knew them off by heart. Dad left her at the gate.

She had to enter the school by the main door, cross the vestibule to the hall, take a seat in there with the other First Years, and wait. *You will be allocated your form,* the instructions had said. Form, she realised, was the Grammar School word for 'class', just like in the stories she read.

When she took a seat, quite a few new pupils were already in the hall. Two girls settled on either side of her. Neither spoke. Nor did she.

Names were called for Form 1. Martha Dobson was not among them. She began to feel hot in her new regulation navy gabardine raincoat. Form 1A was called. Still her name was not listed. She began to wonder if her presence there was a huge mistake.

Those who remained were form 1B. Mr Shepherd was to be their form teacher. With relief, Mattie finally heard her own name. Mr Shepherd told them where to find cloakrooms in which to hang their coats and how to reach their form room where he allowed them to choose their seats. The desks were all singles. Mattie opted for one by the window, overlooking the playing fields and woods and fields that stretched to the edge of Sittendon. Mr Shepherd gave them their timetables to copy, with a plan of the layout of the school. Mattie liked him. He was more human than the nuns, who had been most of the teachers at St. Angela's. She thought a man teacher would be better for lots of reasons. He was warm and friendly. He could be stern but not scary, like the nuns. Twice he had cause to reprimand someone called Drusilla Parkinson.

"Young lady, I cannot compete with you," he said

the second time. "Will you please cease your chatter and pay attention."

As text books were given out, so were instructions to take them home and cover them.

"What with?" Lola Johnson said.

"Brown paper, at least," was the reply.

Lola made a face. Mattie's heart sank. Brown paper cost money. Mum would grumble.

At break, like in school stories, not playtime any more, Drusilla Parkinson approached Mattie.

"Will you be my friend? I don't know anyone else, only Barbara, and I don't know her very well. And you look nice."

Drusilla was not Mattie's type. She was what Mattie thought of as posh. This was one of the first things she was becoming aware of as the first day unfolded. Many of the pupils and most of the teachers she would describe in this way. This caused her to see herself as not belonging, possibly not even clever enough to be there. At St. Theresa's, many of the teachers were nuns from Ireland who spoke softly, even when being stern, in which case their voices had become sharp and tight-lipped, not loud and domineering and bossy as some of the Grammar School teachers seemed to be.

"Come along there, girl," one of the men teachers said to her as she wound her way round the crowded corridors. Mattie cringed. She was new and trying to find her way.

Mr Shepherd was kind, with a gentle voice. Mr Barnes, who taught Geography, was not. He, too, needed to speak to Drusilla Parkinson.

"Just take your turn, please," he said in an over-riding voice.

"Sorry, sir," Drusilla said, confident in her own Gracehill voice and still getting the attention she so rightfully deserved.

In History, which was starting with the ancient Greeks, Miss Willoughby, tweedy, no fuss, but with exaggerated vowels, asked for the name of some of the gods. Mattie's hand went up.

"Yes?" A long finger pointed to her, arched-eyebrows were raised.

Mattie cleared her throat. "Apollo" came her answer in a whisper.

"Speak up, child," Miss Willoughby said.

Try as she did, all that came out was a hoarse whisper. "Apollo."

"Did you say 'Apollo'?"

"Yes, Miss Willoughby," but Miss Willoughby probably did not hear.

Miss Willoughby had to be addressed by her name, not 'Miss', as Lola Johnson had done and been put in her place by that haughty voice. Not that Lola cared much. Mattie reminded herself that, had she been able to go to a girls' boarding school, like in Libby's books, this was how it would have been.

* * *

"So how did you get on?"

Mum was waiting when Mattie burst through the scullery door into the kitchen.

"All right."

"Did you like it?"

"I've got three new friends." Mattie pulled off her new regulation raincoat and threw it over the back of a chair.

"You can hang that up," Mum said.

"In a minute." Mattie held out three fingers of her left hand. "There's Drusilla Parkinson. She asked to be my friend. There's Barbara Ellington, who knew her a bit at their primary school, but they weren't friends. They are now. And there's Rosemary Hadlow."

"Oh?" Mum poured tea from the teapot into two cups. "And where does this Drusilla live?"

"Gracehill." It was like admitting to having done something wrong.

"Really?" Mum's lips pursed.

"I don't know where Barbara lives. Rosemary lives in Milton Stanwick. She's nice. I don't know what school she was at. Milton Stanwick primary, I expect. And Lola Johnson. She's a bit scary. You'd say she was common."

Mum passed a cup and saucer over to Mattie. "Keep away from her, then. No one else from St Angela's? Not Carol?"

"No. Only a boy. Conor something. I didn't know him, anyway. I'm in form 1B. Carol's gone to the Sec. Mod."

"1B? Form? Sounds like racing."

"Class. Only posher. And at dinner time we have break not playtime and its lunch break not dinner break. We still get our milk, at break."

"Oh, I see." Mum said. "And the teachers? Can you do the lessons?"

"My form master is Mr Shepherd. He's lovely. We did a bit of French."

"Oh, my! My daughter, learning French." Mum did not smile.

Mattie hung up her raincoat and went upstairs to her bedroom to change out of her school uniform. When she came down to the kitchen again, she asked, "Any news from Libby?"

"No," Mum said.

Mattie stood stock still. "Not even something about me starting at the Grammar School? I had hoped for a letter from her, but a message, out of a letter to you, that would do."

"Oh, she did say, in a brief note last week, that she hoped you would get on all right."

Mattie slumped onto a chair. She picked at her tea. She said little and helped with the washing up as she usually did.

"I'm going out," she announced.

"Where?" said Mum.

"To see Carol."

"Why are you bothering with her now you're at the Grammar School?"

Mattie did not want to explain herself. She had something on her mind.

"Don't you want to tell Dad all about it when he comes home?"

Mattie hovered on the threshold of the back door. "Yes. I won't be long."

Carol lived ten minutes away, on a small, mature council estate that had been built some thirty years ago after the First World War. Mum hankered after one of these houses, especially a semi-detached one, like Carol's parents had.

Carol was pleased to see her. "I thought you wouldn't bother with me," she said.

"I told you. You are still my best friend. I want to ask you something. It's private."

Carol's face lit up. "What about?"

"I'll tell you. Where can we go where it's quiet?"

"The shed."

Carol led the way down the long, narrow garden, past potatoes, onions, carrots, cabbages, past a soft fruit garden, right to the end into a small orchard, of half a dozen fruit trees, in the corner of which stood a shed. Dad never bothered with their garden, maybe because he worked in Parks and Gardens and had enough of digging and planting by the time he came home at night.

"In here," Carol said, opening the door wide.

The shed was warm inside and smelled of sacking, a dry, dusty smell. Carol arranged a grubby old blanket on the earth floor. "Tell," she said, squatting on the blanket.

Mattie lowered herself opposite her. "It's about my sister, Libby," she said.

"Has something happened?"

"No. Nothing's happened. That's the trouble. I thought she'd write to me, starting a new school, you know?" She was reluctant to use the words 'Grammar School', in case Carol saw it as showing off. "But she hasn't. At least, Mum said Libby hoped I'd get on okay. That's not much, is it?"

"Why can't you write to her?"

"No address. I told you. Mum said I could put a note in her letter. I did, but she hasn't answered."

"You'll just have to ask. Outright. No pussy-footing."

"You don't know my mother."

"Just ask. Outright. You know, as though you mean it. Then," and Carol became really animated, "you can come back to me and tell me."

"Right. I will. I'll look for a good opportunity. And

I'll tell you. In a couple of days. How did you get on at Sit Sec Mod?"

"Oh, you know. It's school. What about you?"

"Yeah. It's school. With knobs on. I'm scared I'll do something wrong."

Carol grinned.

Mattie considered Carol's advice. She came home from school one evening at the beginning of the second week of term, pleased with herself and how she was doing at the Grammar School. She was excited about French and her English teacher, Mrs Andrews, expressed approval of her essay, (not 'composition' now), on 'How I would spend Fifty Pounds'. Mattie had written that she would search for her sister whose whereabouts were unknown to her and buy a milk shake for her friend Carol who had not got to the Grammar School but was still going to be her best friend. She realised it would be wise not to tell Mum about the essay, especially about how she would spend fifty pounds. Nothing had been said but Libby and her whereabouts were clearly not for discussion. Fired by Mrs Andrews' praise, she felt ready to talk to Mum as Carol had suggested.

"As though you mean it," Carol had said.

Coming downstairs, having changed out of her school uniform, she breezed into the kitchen, her notebook in one hand, a pencil in the other.

"Mum, I'm writing to Libby about my school. Can I have her address, please?"

Mum, at the kitchen table with a cup of tea, looked up.

"No," she said. "I'm afraid you can't."

"Why not?" Mattie said, meaning it

26

"I'm not giving it to you."

"Why not?"

"I don't want you to have it."

"Why not?" Mattie wished she could think of another way of meaning it.

"Libby doesn't want you to have it."

"That's not true. It can't be true. Libby would never cut off from me like that."

"Well, she has."

Mattie took a deep breath and Mum heard it.

"Before you ask again," Mum said, "The answer is 'no'. And it always will be. I've already told you, you can give me a note for her and I will send it with mine."

There was that straight-lined mouth look on Mum's face. Mattie, about to shout "Why?" thought better of it. The word came out in a humble "Why? Tell me why, Mum?"

"There is to be no discussion on the subject. Here's your tea. Drink it up and stop trying to make waves."

The cup and saucer were passed to her. Stunned, Mattie sat down at the table.

"It's not fair," she began but knew it was useless. There was nothing she could do, except see Carol. At least she had that support.

So that was what she did. She ate her tea and walked out into the now cooling evening air. It was strange, she reflected, that she had wanted to see Libby in order to talk about Carol being upset at the Grammar School spoiling their friendship. Now she was on her way to see Carol because she was unable to contact Libby about anything private.

They sat on the floor of the shed again. Carol had

taken an apple, for each of them, from the store of apples at the back of the shed.

"I'll give you some onions for your Mum if you like," she said. "There's loads of them over there."

"No thanks." Mattie bit into her apple. "I don't want her to know where I've been." Her voice was indistinct over the apple. "I had a bit of a disagreement with her. That's why I'm here."

"Your sister?"

Mattie recounted the conversation with her mother. "You see, she refuses, absolutely refuses, you know, to give me Libby's address and she won't explain, either."

"It sounds fishy to me," Carol said.

"It's beginning to sound fishy to me."

"Is she in prison?"

"I hope not! That's a shocking idea."

"Perhaps she's abroad."

"You can get stamps for letters abroad."

"Perhaps she's married."

"So what? I could still speak to my sister."

"Perhaps she's ill."

"Don't say that. She would want me to write if she was ill."

"I can't think of anything else. I don't know what you can do, either."

"She says, Mum does, that I can put a note in her letter to Libby."

"That means she knows the address, doesn't it? She must have it written down somewhere."

Mattie shrugged. "I can't really search for it, can I?"

"Why not? I would. In her handbag, for a start."

"You're wicked. I can't do that. If I got caught..."

"That'd show her."

"She never goes out, except to the Council Offices, and that's when I'm at school."

"What about asking your Dad?"

* * *

At Mass one Sunday, shortly after Mattie's second shed-meeting with Carol, Father Tully was in a fierce mood when he spoke from the pulpit. He dwelt for ages on the necessity of a good education.

"And I mean good. You get the best education in a Catholic school. It has come to my notice that some pupils, formerly from St Angela's, have opted to go to a non-Catholic Grammar School. For the sake of a ten mile journey, to the next town, where there are good Catholic Grammar and secondary modern schools for the girls, all in one, St Catherine's, and for the boys, the Christian Brothers, these pupils could have been saved from the risk to their immortal souls. There are communist teachers at the Grammar School here. Communists, as we all know, are atheists. They don't believe in God. Imagine putting your child at such a risk."

Mattie could not understand what he meant. What was a communist and what was the other thing that communists were? And why didn't he attack people like Carol's parents who sent their children to the secondary modern school? She would have to wait until she got home to ask about this. Her parents never attended Mass.

"I'm a mother," Mum had said once on being questioned by Frank after he had seen his best friend with his parents at Mass. "I have a dispensation." At this, Dad had laughed out loud. He was a not a very convinced convert to the Catholic faith, so he stayed at home too.

Today, on their way home from Mass, Frank was ready to goad Mattie about the evil teachers at the Grammar School.

"You'll have to go to confession, Mattie."

"I will not. Going to school is not a sin."

"Yes, you will. You should have gone to St Catherine's in Ammerfield. No boys, there, no commies either."

"Commies?"

"Communists," Frank said kicking clods of earth in the gutter.

"So where will you go, if you get the scholarship?"

"The Christian Brothers in Ammerfield."

"They beat you there," Mattie said with confidence. It was a well-known fact.

Mattie had a problem. How on earth was she to ask her father anything without her mother overhearing? She reported back to Carol, mostly on Saturdays when they went into the town together, not to shop, but to see and be seen by their friends, both from their old schools and their new schools.

The time passed swiftly, both at school and at home. There was no news of Libby and no mention of her. Nor was there any opportunity for Mattie to speak to Dad. As for school, it might be a Grammar School, but it was still a school and aside from a few differences, like separate subject teachers, the strict uniform rules, forms instead of classes and lunch breaks instead of dinner playtime, it required the same application and obedience that St Angela's had. There were new subjects, like arithmetic which was now maths and divided into arithmetic, geometry and the dreaded algebra, and science consisted of biology, chemistry and physics. There was also something called domestic science, and gym, in the gym, which was a weird and alarming place. Imagine, actually being told to climb the ropes. The whole atmosphere was serious, formal and laughter was for breaks. There was also ink. Ink wells were mysteriously filled over-night and the boys, and Lola Johnson, would, on occasions, flick inky blotting-paper pellets at the girls, in some cases ruining good quality, white blouses. Drusilla Parkinson was a frequent target.

It was not until the October half term holiday, six weeks after starting at the Grammar School that Mattie had an opportunity to speak to Dad without Mum being able to hear. She and Carol had gone to the park. Carol spotted him first.

She pointed excitedly. "There he is."

"Who?"

"Your Dad."

And it was Dad. Carol was pointing to a mower being ridden by a man in dark boiler-suit with council initials, SBC, for Sittendon Borough Council, emblazoned on his back.

"So it is. I don't often see him at work."

"You can ask him now, can't you?"

Mattie hesitated. She had no doubt about Carol's meaning. Since her friend had first suggested it, the subject had been mentioned at least once each time they met.

"Go on," Carol urged.

Mattie paused for an instant, before running across

the grass, waving to him. He caught sight of her and slowed down his mower to a standstill to sit on it while it chugged as though annoyed at being stopped. He waited for her to reach him.

"Hallo, there," he said. "What are you up to?"

"Dad," she panted. "Dad, listen. I want to ask you a question." She had to warn him, it was only fair.

"Go on, then."

"I want to write to Libby and Mum won't let me have her address."

"Well, if that's what she says, you'll have to abide by it."

"But, Dad, it's not fair. Why won't she let me have it?"

"Can't you put a letter in with hers?"

"I have, but I don't get a reply. Can't you make her tell me?"

"Do you want to say something you don't want Mum to see?"

"Yes." The original problem had been about Carol but that was more or less solved now. "I think Mum just wants to read what I say."

"I can't make her do what you want. You shouldn't be asking that. I'm sorry. You'll have to do what Mum says."

"Suppose she doesn't post it?"

"Your Mum wouldn't do a trick like that. Now, I have to go and get on. Just accept what Mum says, there's a good girl. It's not like you to try to create trouble. Be good." And he let out the throttle and the mower engine roared with energy and Dad chugged on his way.

* * *

The biggest occasions on the school calendar in the Autumn term were the Christmas Carol Concert and the Christmas parties.

"Each year has a party," Mattie explained to Mum. "Even the Fifth Year and the Sixth Form. The First Years' party is the earliest. All the girls are talking about what they're going to wear."

"In October? Before half-term?"

After this, Mattie decided it was best not to mention the issue for a long while. What Mum wanted to talk about now was the weather.

"It's turned cold," Mum said. "Why don't you wear the hat, gloves and scarf that Grandma has knitted for you?"

"I can't," Mattie said. "They're not uniform."

"What are you supposed to do then, freeze?"

"I need a beret and a school scarf. I suppose I can wear Grandma's mittens."

"It's never-ending, this uniform business. I knew it would be like this."

"I'll have them for Christmas, then."

"You'll have to. You can't have these things as well as presents."

Weeks later, Mattie dared to mention the Christmas party.

"You'll just have to wear one of Libby's old dresses," Mum said.

Mattie didn't argue. One of Libby's old dresses was at least a solution, even if it was too big. But events altered even that plan for the party. Not long before Christmas, Grandma died. One afternoon, Mattie arrived home from school to find the kitchen full of relatives. There was Aunt Delia and cousins Paddy and Fidelma and other aunts and uncles rarely seen except on such occasions. Grandma had died in her sleep.

There were several aspects to Grandma's demise. Mattie's first thought was that she would not be the victim of any more ghastly hand-knitted woollens to make her itch. Then it turned out that the funeral was to be held on the day of the First Years' Christmas party.

"It's my school party day," she said when she was told in front of the family.

"You'll be going to no parties on the day of your Grandmother's funeral," Mum said.

"Only to the wake," Aunt Delia said with satisfaction. She was ill-at-ease about her niece being at the Grammar School, Mattie knew it. Delia behaved as though Mattie had done something embarrassing.

"Why can't I go? We've all been talking about it for ages."

"It would be disrespectful, that's why."

"That's silly. Grandma wouldn't want me to miss the party because of her. You've even got me silver sandals from the WVS."

"Look at her there, Rita," Delia said, "standing in her gym slip like she was at a private school or something. Does she not know what Father Tully thinks of the Grammar School? You know, some of the teachers there are communists. What kind of respect is it for Grandma, you wanting to consort with atheists?"

"What would they think of you, at your school?" Mum was emboldened by her sister's remarks. "Partying on your Grandma's funeral day?"

"I wouldn't tell them."

34

"Wouldn't tell them, indeed! Are you listening to yourself?" Delia was shocked.

Mattie summoned every ounce of disobedience she had ever possessed. She raised her voice. "I want to go to the party. It's not fair."

"This Grammar School, it's got like a religion," Mum said. "Go to your room, Mattie."

Mattie went to her room, stamping on every one of the stairs of the two flights to the top. She sat on her bed. The dream would have to be relinquished. She had no dress to impress, anyway. It would be as well to accept the defeat.

She went to the wake, the never ending party around Grandma's open coffin in the sitting-room of the old people's bungalow where she had lived on the new estate. The wake had good things about it. Everyone made a fuss of Mattie, not just because she had a place at the Grammar School but because most of the family thought she was a nice girl and what a pity it was she missed her school party. That showed Delia. Libby did not attend the funeral. Mattie had been hoping she would come. She overheard Delia say something that made her cross.

"I was thinking Libby might be here," Delia said to Mum. "I was after giving her a piece of my mind."

"Well, I'm sure glad you never had the chance, Delia. It's very upsetting, you know."

"You didn't tell Mum, then?"

"I did not. Delia, hush, will you?" Mattie had moved from the shadows.

There was a lot of food at the wake and some rows, too.

"Will you look at them fellas, Rita," Delia said, far

from sober herself. "Drunk as lords. Will you give us a hand at dealing with them?"

Dealing with them meant persuading them to leave, which they did after a lot of protesting.

"Uncle Kevin and Uncle Seamus always get drunk," Mattie said after Mum and Delia had thrown them out and they were dusting their hands triumphantly. "You know that." Mum was strict about men drinking. She was strict about a lot of things.

Later, there were the squabbles about Grandma's possessions.

"Mattie, there's a whole load of hand-knitted woolly jumpers and things that Grandma knitted for you," Mum said. "She obviously didn't expect to die, poor soul, because she put them all aside for future Christmases. She'll never be seeing them on you."

Mattie wanted to pass them on to Fidelma, who turned her nose up at them, saying they were childish. The truth was, Mattie decided, Fidelma was getting fat. She had made a real pig of herself at the wake.

It was not just the jumpers for Mattie that Grandma had left.

"I want the Belleek pottery," Mum said, much to Delia's chagrin. Delia got the Belleek and Mum was left with Irish linen tablecloths and tea towels, piles of them.

"Oh, Jesus, Rita, look what your Frank is doing," Delia said to distract Mum from the victory.

Frank was discovering Guinness and Mattie guessed what his future might hold. Then there was the dancing and singing. Oh, what a send off old Fionnuala McQuaid had! The funeral Mass was sombre, with black vestments and Father Tully in his grimmest element.

The flowers spilled over the grave in respectable mountains.

Then life resumed normality without Grandma.

"'Tis a big hole she's left in our lives, sure enough," Delia said.

Mattie went back to school the day after the funeral to sympathy and commiserations from her form-mates. The party had been wonderful, she was told.

"And Drusilla Parkinson's dress was just too much," Rosemary Hadlow confided. "Everyone says so."

The truth about Drusilla Parkinson was she was too fond of herself and the form members were becoming tired of her.

* * *

Delia's comments about Libby had irked Mattie, so had the reference to communist teachers. Some days after the funeral she decided to ask her father about communists.

The family was having Sunday lunch. Quite often Dad would regale his children with carefully edited versions of his exploits as a soldier in World War I. He would speak of mud, the trenches, of exploding shells and singing '*Mademoiselle from Armentieres*'. Mattie broke in to change the subject.

"Dad, what is a communist?"

Everyone looked at her.

"A communist," Dad said, "is someone who is a member of the Communist Party." He loved to talk. He seemed pleased to have been asked a question.

"Are they bad?"

"Well, they can be. Russia is a communist country."

"A whole country? Are they all bad?"

37

"They want world domination. You know, to be in charge of the whole world. They kill people who don't agree with them."

Mattie put down her knife and fork. "Kill people? Are there any people here in England who are communists?"

"Yes, of course."

"Do we let them live here?"

"It's a party. A political party."

"Are they dangerous?"

"Eat your dinner," Mum said, "and stop thinking about things above you."

"No, they're not dangerous, not like robbers," Dad said. "Just dangerous thinking, that's all. Has Father Tully been ranting?"

"Not today. Aunt Delia said something about communist teachers at the Grammar School. And I've heard it from other people. Father Tully said another word about them."

"Did he say atheists? Father Tully would not like communists because they are atheists. You don't have to take any notice of him. He's got a bee in his bonnet about communists. I expect the Sunday collections are dropping."

"George!" Mum said.

Mattie was satisfied with the answers to her questions about communists. But the remark made by Delia, about Libby not being at the funeral, also burned in her thoughts. Delia had wanted to give Libby 'a piece of her mind', which was an expression for telling off people who had done something wrong. What had Libby done wrong and why had Mum said it was 'very upsetting'?

Mattie went to speak to Carol about this development. It was too cold to sit in the shed now, so they sat in Carol's untidy bedroom. Her bed was unmade, clothes were flung thoughtlessly over a chair, the hairbrush had more of Carol's wispy blonde hair than was on her head.

"So," Carol said, "she's done something wrong." Carol was hoping for excitement. She wanted life to be like in the pictures, dramatic, sensational.

"And Aunt Delia knows about it and I don't. That's not fair."

"You've got to look for an address," Carol said. "That's all there is now. But there will surely be a Christmas card from Libby, won't there, to your parents, even if you don't get one. See if you can get to the post first."

"Mum will suspect if I suddenly go rushing after the post."

"Not if you make out you're ever so excited about Christmas."

* * *

Christmas could never be exciting for the Dobson family. There was not enough money for necessities at any time of the year. If it was cold, extra money for coal had to be found and as it had snowed a little before Christmas this year, even necessities needed to be limited. Mum did her best, making cakes, puddings, thinking of presents to make. No one was disappointed because no one expected a lot.

"The war has been over only five years," Dad said this year. "It'll take time. Most people are in the same situation. It will be better when there are things in the shops."

Mattie thought that a strange comment. There were things in the shops now. There always had been, as far as she could remember.

The Christmas post, monitored as rigorously as Mattie was able, had yielded nothing. There was not even a card from Libby, not for anyone. Mattie could have cried. It was Christmas and Libby was not there. Paper chains had to be made without the supervision of her sister, as, alone, she folded and glued loops of coloured paper during a gloomy afternoon. Holly, from the lanes outside the town was, this year, gathered with Frank's hindrance, not Libby's help. The puddings were made and stirred. They contained mostly breadcrumbs as there were still shortages. Icing for the cake was made with soya flour, flavoured with almond essence, as Mum complained about shortages and spoke about 'real marzipan'. Stockings, really Dad's socks, were hung on Christmas Eve, Mattie aware of the empty bed that had no stocking, in her room. Frank and Tony were awake at five o'clock, thrilled by cheap toys from Woolworths, a homemade cracker, one chocolate, a few boiled sweets, an orange, an apple and a sixpence in each of their stockings. Mattie could hardly be bothered to look in hers. The Christmas dinner was of roast beef, traditional, with Brussels sprouts, swede, carrots and parsnips. Everyone settled at three o'clock to hear the King's broadcast on the wireless. Presents were even fewer without Libby's contributions and were mostly hankies, socks, useful things.

In the limbo days after Christmas and before the fleeting celebrations of the New Year, she went into the town centre to search the library for the latest Elsie Oxenham book about the Abbey Girls. This was a writer whom Mum recalled reading when she was young. On entering the children's library, Mattie saw Barbara Ellington there, seated at a table, engrossed in a book.

"Hello, Barbara," Mattie greeted her in a library whisper. "Did you have a good Christmas?"

"Lovely, thank you." Barbara glanced up at her and Mattie pulled out a chair to sit next to her.

"What did you get?"

"Oh, riding lessons. That was what I wanted. I have a pony, you know. Mummy and Daddy bought it for me as a reward for getting a place at the Grammar."

"Really? Lucky you. Just like in a book. I don't even have a cat."

"No?" Barbara looked her up and down. Mattie grew aware that she was wearing her regulation navy blue gabardine school raincoat with Grandma's last tea-cosy woolly hat and mittens. Barbara had on a brown tweed coat with the brown beret to match. And leather gloves.

Mattie stuffed her mittens into her raincoat pockets. "Are you looking forward to going back to school?"

"Yes, I suppose. It's hard work, though, isn't it?"

"Algebra is," Mattie said.

"It all is. Mummy has to stand over me to make sure I do my homework. I would leave it otherwise. It's hard, most of it."

"My Mum doesn't."

"It's because she cares, Mummy says."

"Barbara?" A whispered command came from among the bookshelves.

"Coming, Mummy." Barbara stood to push back her chair. "I've got to go."

Mattie caught sight of Barbara's Mummy, a tall

woman in a fur coat. She wore pearl earrings. There was an aura about her, a shine. It was her hair, perhaps, which was permed and glossy. Her lipstick was bright. She stood upright, very upright. Mother and daughter left the library but not before Mattie had heard the low voiced exchange.

"Who was that, Barbara?"

"Mattie Dobson. From school."

"The Grammar School? Why is she wearing her school raincoat in the holidays…?"

Mattie glanced down at the school raincoat. It had cost a lot of money.

"Wear it," Mum had said, "and get the value out of it. You're bound to grow out of it before long."

This was impossible to imagine, growing out of the raincoat. Now it was enormous and very long. Mattie tightened the belt to make it look as if it fitted. She wished she had a best coat as well.

CHAPTER THREE

After Christmas, Mattie was aware that the new term, the Spring term, did not create the same level of enthusiasm in her as the Autumn term had. She woke late for the first day back at school and needed to rush her breakfast and run all the way. Double maths was the first lesson of the year and this included algebra. She found algebra a complete mystery.

The days were cold, the house was never warm enough. On some mornings,

Mattie would wake to find her bedroom window covered with fern patterns in ice. Libby used to breathe on them to make a hole so she could see the whiteness of the frost on the fields beyond the garden. Mattie thought that was a waste of beauty.

As winter turned into Spring, the number of meetings with Carol to talk about Libby diminished, largely due to the shed being nowhere near as comfortable as it had been in the Autumn. Saturdays in the town were less frequent, too, as they were finding less and less to talk about and Mattie's preoccupation with Libby's departure waned.

"I know all the nicknames of the teachers now," Mattie told Carol. "There's Taffy Jones, Taffy Williams, Taffy Roberts and Spud."

"What's Taffy? Is it their names?"

They were passing a stall on the market that sold underwear, blatantly.

"No, it's because they're Welsh."

"Oh." Carol was not really interested.

"And the two women science teachers live together."

"What's interesting about that?"

It was no use trying to explain the gossip to Carol. She was only interested in clothes.

* * *

Mattie's birthday was at the end of April. She was twelve. It seemed to be a great age. The Summer term began soon after with a requirement for a summer dress, a blazer and a panama hat.

"You'll have to have them for your birthday," Mum said. "I can't afford them otherwise. The grant money didn't cover everything."

So Mattie went to school on a breezy morning dressed in her new summer uniform, looking just like everyone else at Sittendon Grammar School, but convinced she was the only pupil who could not understand algebra.

When May came, she registered that a year had passed since Libby had left. A year was a long time, it was one twelfth of her life.

* * *

Early in the summer term, after a difficult day that included working with Drusilla as a partner in the gym and a maths lesson in which algebra had become less of a mystery and more of a horror, Mattie emerged from school, weary. Crowds of pupils milled round the gates, as always, blocking the way. The bright sunny day had fired their energy. They were noisy and high-spirited. Mattie pushed her way out, then, further along the road she spied a familiar figure standing on the pavement. She stopped in her tracks. It looked so like Libby.

She must be imagining things. It was because she was tired. A wave of panic washed over her. Was it a ghost? Was Libby dead? Was it a hallucination? Everything was unreal. Someone pushed her from behind. She was in the way. Her satchel was heavy all of a sudden as she stumbled forward, staring at the pale figure ahead of her.

It was Libby and she had seen her. Half expecting the vision to vanish, Mattie moved towards her, clutching her satchel under one arm, her other arm stretched out.

Yes, it definitely was Libby, a changed Libby, though, thinner, more anxious-looking, pale, her hair, once glossy, now short and unkempt.

Mattie's hand touched Libby's arm.

"Libby!" Mattie said hoarsely. "It is you? Are you real?"

"Mattie." Libby was smiling and she hugged her and kissed her cheek. "How's school?"

"Okay." School was dismissed. "Where have you been? Are you coming home? I've so missed you."

"I've missed you, Mattie. I've missed you, too. I mustn't stay long. And I don't want you to mention at home that you've seen me. Is that all right with you? To keep quiet about you seeing me? Please? Promise?"

Mattie nodded vigorously. "Promise." She would to agree to anything to please her sister after not seeing her for so long.

"I know it's wrong of me to ask. But I so wanted to

see you. You must tell no one, no one at all, do you understand?"

"Yes. Have you been in prison? I wouldn't care if you had, honest. Are you ill? Did you get my poems?"

"Poems?"

Mattie came alive. "I knew it! I knew it. Mum, she didn't even send them, did she? She didn't even send my poems to you."

"She thinks she's protecting you. It doesn't matter. And no, I haven't been in prison and I'm not ill. I'm so sorry leaving like that. I had no choice."

"I don't understand."

"No, and I can't explain right now. I mustn't be long. I don't want anyone I knew to see me. Mattie, do you get any pocket money?"

"Not very often. Why? I've still got the ten shilling note I found on the dressing table the day you left. I couldn't bear to spend it. Why?"

"Bus fare. Can you get to Ammerfield on Saturday morning?"

"To see you? Yes, yes. Of course I can."

"There is a cafe in the bus station. I'll meet you there. This coming Saturday."

Mattie gazed at her. Next Saturday she and Carol had planned to go round the market in Sittendon. Carol would have to be let down on this occasion. "What time?"

"Eleven o'clock?"

"Great. Libby, where have you been?"

"We'll talk then. How are Mum and Dad?"

"Mum's the usual."

"You have to remember she's not well."

"And Dad's the same. Always calm."

"And the boys?"

"They get on my nerves."

"And the Grammar School. Do you like it there?"

"Yes, I do. Did Mum tell you I got in?"

"Yes. Nearly a year ago. But I don't hear from her now. She doesn't write to me any more. I've got to go, Mattie."

"Already?"

"Yes. Be good, Mattie, apart from the not telling. And I'm sorry I left like that but I had no choice."

Mattie nodded, unable to speak because Libby was going. And with another hug and a kiss on the cheek, Libby turned and walked away, looking back only once to wave.

* * *

Summer at the Grammar School was unexpectedly different from the rest of the year. It was not only the uniform that was different, although the boys did not have an equivalent to summer dresses, just the blazers and the boys' version of panama hats. The sports were different. Netball and hockey gave way to tennis, rounders and athletics. The boys played cricket, for which they needed white flannels. The girls were supposed to have whites and white plimsolls for tennis but it soon became apparent, after two weeks of agonising on Mattie's part, that that applied only to those who were really keen and good at tennis. Mum visited the WVS again so she was provided with white plimsolls that had to be 'blanco-ed' every week.

During tennis lessons, the opportunity to sit on the grass and talk, if the weather was fine, presented itself. Drusilla and Barbara talked about what they would do when they left school. With Rosemary, Mattie sat on the grass, all four being less than competent at tennis and therefore knocked out early.

"I want to stay on at school until I'm eighteen," Drusilla said, gazing up at the sky as they all lay on their backs, "and go to university."

Mattie had no idea what university was, only that the word cropped up occasionally to mystify her. She didn't care much, either. She was looking forward to Saturday. The prospect of having a long talk with Libby filled every space in her mind, even displacing the anxiety about algebra.

"What will you study?" Barbara said. "I want to do history. I just love history."

"Oh, no, not history," Drusilla said. "I might go to teacher training college. I want to be a teacher. What about you, Mattie?"

"I don't really know. I do like French."

"You could be a teacher, too," Barbara said. "A French teacher."

Mattie was pensive. Surely you did not learn French in order to teach French? There must be another reason for learning French.

"Or a translator," Barbara said. "Or a courier. Or work in an embassy."

Mattie sat up. "So I could. But it's a long way away, all that, isn't it?"

"You'd have to get enough O-levels. In other subjects too."

"Oh, yes, of course," Mattie said. She didn't know what O-levels were, either. She had heard about them but did not like to ask her friends what they were. And she didn't know who else to ask.

48

"What about you, Rosemary?" Drusilla said.

"What are O-levels?" Rosemary said.

Drusilla and Barbara both sat up and burst out laughing. Rosemary's pretty face grew scarlet. She propped herself up on one elbow, her brown eyes watery.

"Exams, you twerp," Drusilla said. "In the Fifth Year. When you're sixteen. After two years in the Sixth Form you do A-levels. If you pass, you can go to university or teacher training college. If you don't get O-levels and A-levels, you become a skivvy."

Mattie jumped to her feet. Surely Libby was not a skivvy. Mum had used that word about her once. "Let's go for a walk, Rosie. I'm tired of talking about the future. I'm finding the present difficult enough. And anyway, the grass is prickly to sit on."

Without another word, Rosemary leapt to her feet. Mattie led the way to a shady spot under some trees, where Miss Grumble, the nickname for Miss Humble, the games mistress, could not see them. A shy arm tucked into hers. Rosemary smiled up at her.

"She is so rude, Drusilla," Rosemary said, chopping the short, dry grass with her tennis racket. "Just because she lives on Gracehill doesn't mean she can say what she likes."

Mattie said nothing. Mum had always warned her not to gossip about other people even if they were really unpleasant. She would have loved to unleash the vehemence she felt towards Drusilla and Barbara at that moment.

"I'm sure she didn't mean it," she said.

"Of course she meant it. She loves putting us both down. What did you mean when you said you found the present difficult?"

"Algebra. I hate it. I don't know what it is, what it's for."

"It's for O-levels. Everything is for O-levels. I see it now." Rosemary paused, regarding Mattie with a sad expression. "No one ever told me. She's quite right Drusilla. I am a twerp."

* * *

On Saturday morning, Mattie was up and about early. Carol had long gone completely from her thoughts. With the ten shilling note clasped in her hand, and her poems and pictures folded in one of her dress pockets, she set out for the bus stop, making a short diversion to a general store where she bought this week's 'Girls' Crystal', her favourite girls' magazine. A ten shilling note would be too much for a bus fare. That cost eightpence. 'Girls' Crystal' often had stories about boarding schools. She wanted to buy a present for Libby, too, but so much in the store was still on the ration and Mum kept all the ration books.

The change from the ten shilling note was heavy in the pocket of her dress as she boarded the bus. The journey to Ammerfield lasted for over half an hour. Until today, she had made only a few bus journeys on her own. Once she had gone to Aunt Delia's, who lived in Stanford Grange, twenty miles away and whose husband, Uncle Kevin, had a car. Once she'd had to catch a bus to the other side of Sittendon when Mum had been in the hospital for a few days. Otherwise this was a big adventure, even bigger when she thought of the reason for it.

She arrived early at Ammerfield.

The cafe in the bus station was easy to spot, right near the way out. She attempted to brave the world outside the bus station only to hurry back to the cafe, still too early.

Inside it was hot, steamy and smoky. The customers were mostly men who made a lot of noise, talking loudly and laughing. The place was not comfortable for her. In a gloomy corner was a small table for two, a place as safe as she would feel in there, so she made for it. She ordered a cup of tea and, to eat, a penny bun, soft, fresh and sticky on top

And she waited.

The hands of the clock on the wall of the cafe crept slowly round. At eleven o'clock, her whole body was tense and alert, her eyes skimming the place, inside and out, ears waiting for the familiar voice calling her name.

The minutes passed. The clock showed five past eleven, then ten past. She tried not to look at it. At a quarter past, she began to doubt that Libby would appear. At half-past, she was certain she would not. She wanted to cry. She ordered another cup of tea but when it came, was unable to drink it. Her throat was tight.

At midday, she gave up, left the cafe and caught the next bus home. She dragged her disappointed self to Honeyhill Street. The back door was open. Hardly had she crossed the threshold than the words were at her.

"Where have you been?" Mum spoke with anger and with deadly clarity.

Mattie stood still. She should have rehearsed this, not spent her time filling her mind with excuses for Libby.

"Carol's," she said.

Mum came over to her. She sniffed, more than once.

"What?" Mattie said.

"You have not been to Carol's."

"Yes, I have. I told you. Yesterday."

"Don't lie to me."

"I'm not."

"Where have you been?"

"I've been to Carol's."

"Oh no, you haven't. Carol has been round here, looking for you."

The bottom fell out of Mattie's world with a feeling like going down in the lift, very fast, leaving her weak. She said nothing. Carol, here? She'd forgotten about Carol.

Mum began sniffing again. "You smell of cigarette smoke."

"Do I? It must be because I sat upstairs on the bus."

"Bus? What bus?"

Double-deckers only ran to Ammerfield. Now Mum knew.

"The Ammerfield bus."

"Have you been meeting boys? If you have, I'll tan your hide till you can't sit down."

Mattie was still standing in the doorway. She stepped right into the kitchen.

"Well? Have you?" Mum pushed past her to reach the big, bleached wooden spoon on top of the copper in the scullery. Mattie darted for a corner across the kitchen, behind Dad's chair. Mum came back in, brandishing her weapon.

"You've got above yourself since you've been at that Grammar School."

"I thought that was the idea, to better myself."

Now Mum was beside herself. Mattie ducked behind

the chair. Then she had second thoughts. Anything, so long as Mum didn't mention Libby.

She came out of her hiding place, stood looking Mum in the eye. Mum was not well, Libby had said.

"I've got gym on Monday. Someone will see the bruises." As she said it, she noticed her mother's over-stuffed handbag squatting on the kitchen table. There was so much in it, the clasp would not close.

"I'll be taking you down to the Presbytery, to see Father Tully."

"What for?" The exchanges were calmer now.

"Seeing boys. At your age. He'll give you a good talking to."

"You could do that, talk to me. Why don't you?" Mattie took further steps towards the handbag. "Go on, talk to me." She was close to the table now. She reached for the bag, and turned it upside down. The contents scattered over the table and spilled onto the floor.

"You wicked girl. You can pick that up, now. You know I can't bend."

"I'll pick it up if you promise not to hit me with that."

Mum did not reply. Mattie turned to look at her. She was white faced, sad-looking. Then Mattie gave her attention to the contents of the handbag, on the table and on the floor. Two letters, had tumbled out, one was on the table, one on the floor. She stooped to the one on the floor to pick it up. It was typed and the address on the back made it clear it was from the hospital. She collected several more items and put them on the table. There were five ration books and identity cards, several *in memoriam* cards for Fionnuala McQuaid, Grandma, who had died before Christmas, pencils, a powder compact, a lipstick, reading glasses, coins galore, hair pins, earrings, keys and a purse. Nothing of any interest, nothing that could indicate Libby's whereabouts. That handbag followed Mum around, and, as she had once told Mattie, was close to her all the time since during the war, in case of bombing. Throwing the contents about like this was an undaughterly act, a disrespectful act. The seriousness of what she had done was slowly dawning on Mattie.

She placed the last of the contents on the table, taking the chance to check the other envelope. It was only about the application for a council house.

Mum was sitting in Dad's chair, her head in her hands. The wooden spoon lay, forgotten by her feet.

"Sorry, Mum," Mattie said, shocked now to be feeling sorry for her mother.

"I can't cope," Mum muttered.

"No," Mattie said. "It's all rubbish, you know. You can't stop me seeing friends from school." It was not a lie, it was a statement.

"Poor Carol," Mum said.

"I'll go and see her."

"Don't you want some dinner?" Mum said.

"No, thanks. I had a penny bun."

* * *

Things changed, which was a shame because some things changed for the worse. In the month since Mattie had last seen her, Carol had changed. There had been exams, of course and the concern about Libby and meeting her and keeping it secret, but it was not all Mattie's fault that things had changed between her and Carol.

Carol had had a perm. Her fine, pale hair was now a frizzy mop around her thin face. She wore a bra that had uplift and on her size three feet were high-heeled shoes. Despite the warm weather, she wore stockings and there must be a suspender belt holding them up.

And Carol did not smile.

She had opened the door then stood there, haughtily, looking down at Mattie who was standing on the lowest doorstep.

"I came looking for you," she said.

"I know," Mattie said, wanting desperately to tell her about the row with Mum.

"Your Mum was cross. I'm cross. Why did you let me down? You went off to see your new Grammar School friends, did you?"

"No, it wasn't like that. Carol, I'm ever so sorry."

"I waited ages."

Mattie knew all about waiting ages. She needed to be cross, too, cross with Libby, cross with herself for forgetting Carol. "I'm sorry. Look, can we go and sit in your shed?" The urge to unburden herself, to tell the truth, to explain about Libby, hovered so temptingly.

"Sit in the shed? That's kids' stuff. I'm grown up now. I'll be thirteen in September and in two years after that, I'll be able to leave school. I can't wait. And, anyway, I'm getting a Saturday job in Woolworths."

Mattie gazed up at her. Carol had been her friend since the day they had started school together.

"Get yourself a bra," said Carol, and stepped back to close the door. Mattie found herself staring at the letter box. She stepped down backwards, turned and began her walk home. The Grammar School was a lonely place.

* * *

Mattie dared to mention that she wanted a bra. Mum was not overjoyed to hear this.

"Aren't you a bit young yet?"

"No, all the other girls..." This was a phrase she had already found useful.

Mum sighed. "Oh, well, I suppose I'd better take you to Marks and Spencer."

So Mum took her to Marks and Spencer, and just happened to ask her, on the way, if she knew about periods.

"Oh, yeah. It's all about them in magazines. You know."

"Oh, you mean all that rubbish your sister used to read?"

This was the first time Libby had been referred to even though her name was not used.

"Is it rubbish?"

"Well, I suppose not, in this case."

To Mattie, this rare occasion, shopping with Mum, was a pleasant experience. She arrived home with two bras, or brassieres, as Mum called them, both white because that would not show through the PT shirt.

Towards the end of term there was an outing organised by the school, for the First Years, to the Festival of Britain in London's newly developed South Bank. Mum refused to agree to find the money for this. So Mattie and Rosemary were the only girls in their form, 1B, who weren't going. It seemed that Rosemary's family was not so well-off as Mattie had imagined. Along with Conor Flynn, also from St Angela's, who also did not go, alternative arrangements were made for them to join the Art department for the day. Led by Conor, both girls ignored this and after registration and assembly, all three made their way to the local park.

"I vote," Rosemary said, dancing over the grass, "we sit on the bank of the stream and paddle our feet."

"That's got to be better than Art with the second years." Conor tugged off his regulation brown sandals and short grey socks. He stuck his feet in the ice-cold water.

"Too hot to do lessons," Mattie said. "My Mum would kill me if she knew what I was doing."

"Mine will never know," Conor said. "I never wanted to come here, with all these snobs. My Mum and Dad, they didn't want me to go to the Christian Brothers in Ammerfield to get thrashed. That's why I'm here."

"It's true then?" Mattie said, kicking off her own regulation sandals and peeling off her white socks. "That they get thrashed?"

"Yeah. For everything."

"You're exaggerating. My aunt wants my cousin to go there next year. She says boys need a bit of discipline."

Rosemary laughed aloud and kicked her feet about in the water. "My Mum would say that's what I need, if she could see me now." She leaned back on the bank, her hands behind her head on the grass as she gazed up at the summer-blue sky. "She hasn't met Lola Johnson, has she? She doesn't know what a naughty girl really is. Lola Johnson, she's real bad and always in trouble. You know which one's Lola, don't you, Conor?"

"Yeah. 'course I do. Everyone knows her. She lives on Hill Common estate, she does."

"Is there something wrong with Hill Common estate?" Rosemary asked. "There must be if it has Lola Johnson living on it."

"It's a council estate," Conor said. "New houses. Nice if you can get one."

"My Grandma used to live there."

"Did she die there?" Rosemary said.

"Yes, in her bed."

"Have you decided what you want to do when you leave school, Mattie?" Rosemary hadn't much time for boys or death.

"It's a long time ahead, yet. What about you?"

"I never thought about it until I came to the Grammar School. Now I begin to see, since that day, you know, with Drusilla and Barbara. You sit exams, O-levels and stuff and people want to employ you if you pass. But doing what? Then there's something called a degree."

"What's that?"

"Not sure. I think it's what you do after Sixth Form. What about you, Conor?"

"When I leave school? I want to be a builder, like me Da."

"Do you want to get married, Mattie?" Rosemary said.

"I suppose so. But not to somebody who's poor."

"But will you be happy if you don't get married?"

"I'm not sure you get happy by being married." Mattie thought of her mother, never cheerful, never well. Did she know anyone who was married and looked happy? Certainly not Delia, who was always pregnant and complaining about it.

"What about you, Rosemary?"

"I don't know. Falling in love and all that, it's so embarrassing, isn't it?"

All three agreed that it was, moreover, it was a puzzle as well.

The next day, Friday, was the last Friday of term which would end on the following Wednesday. Instead of assembly, there was a form meeting. This meant staying in the form room and hearing notices and words of advice from Mr Shepherd, their form teacher. The first thing he did was to give them their form positions, for their years' work and their positions based on the recent exams.

Mattie had done well in both her year's work and her exams, especially in English, English literature and French.

"Exam results first," Mr Shepherd said. "French. First, Martha Dobson…"

Then again, "English. First, Kaye Waters, second, Martha Dobson…"

Mattie's positions were high in everything but maths and science and even science was more than half way down the list for both the year's work and for the exams. She was so pleased with what she had achieved that she did not notice what Rosemary had observed when everyone else's results were read out.

"What about Barbara?" Rosemary whispered across the gangway.

"What about her?"

"Not so good in exams."

"Really?"

"Twenty-fifth in English, nineteenth in Maths. Can't remember the others."

Mattie waited a while then turned to glance at

Barbara. She was crying. It seemed that without her mother, Barbara was not quite so clever.

At break, Mr Shepherd asked for Mattie, Rosemary and Conor to remain behind after the rest of the class had left. Mattie feared she knew what this was about, the truanting on the previous day.

He spoke kindly to her at first, congratulating her on her exam and year's results.

"What's the matter for a clever girl like you to come so low in maths and science results?"

Mattie grew scarlet. "I don't know, sir. I don't understand algebra and I've gone off maths altogether, even geometry, which I did like."

"Have you spoken to Mr Watts about your difficulties?"

"No, sir." She stood, hands behind her back, waiting to be told off about the truanting.

"I suggest you speak to him. How can he help if you don't tell him?"

"I don't know, sir. I think I'm not a maths person."

"I see. But I think that is rather a misunderstanding of maths. What do you think maths is about?"

"I think you need it in your life."

"I think maths is about the laws of the universe and their relationships."

"I don't understand, sir."

"Think about a lunar eclipse of the sun. Isn't it an odd coincidence that the moon is the right size and distance from the earth to cover the sun exactly?"

"Do you mean, erm, about God?"

"No." He laughed. "I mean about maths. You ask Mr Watts about it."

"Yes, sir. I will."

"Now, Martha, are you a truanting person? You and your friends here?"

Mattie bent her head lower.

"Where were you yesterday?"

"In the park, sir," volunteered, a frightened Rosemary.

"You could have had a really nice day in the Art room and in the gym, with the Second Years, if you had stayed. Now. Do I have to tell your parents about this?"

Mattie remained mute.

"Please, sir, please don't, sir," Rosemary begged in a shaky voice.

"Will you do it again?"

"Oh, no, sir," they chorused as they knew they were expected to do.

"Off you go, then. Next time, they will be informed. No second chances. Right?"

"Yes, sir. Thank you, sir."

They bustled out of the classroom. Mattie burst into tears.

Every pupil in the school had been given their exam and their year's results. The excitement reached a high pitch as they poured out of the school building and passed through the gates that Friday afternoon.

Still upset that she had spoiled her good record at the Grammar School and that nice Mr Shepherd had reprimanded her about truanting, Mattie was convinced she was the only pupil in the whole school not in good spirits. She and Barbara Ellington, of course, whose Mummy had been revealed as not being quite so clever.

"Mattie!" The voice calling her name was soft but so recognisable and so longed for she thought she was dreaming. She looked round. Difficult to see, amongst all the blue summer uniform dresses, there was Libby in a pale blue dress herself. She was standing right by the school gates, almost at Mattie's shoulder.

"Libby," Mattie said and started to cry.

"Come on, don't cry."

"Why didn't you come? I waited ages." Now she'd started crying she couldn't stop.

"I am so sorry, Mattie. I didn't know what to do. There was no way I could contact you. You see, someone was ill. Someone I look after. It's my job, sort of."

"Your job?" Curiosity caused Mattie's sniffles to cease.

"Yes. I haven't got time to tell you all about it now. Is there some way I can contact you? Without Mum knowing? Mum must not know. Let's walk this way." Libby grasped her by the elbow and propelled her gently along the road, amongst the thinning pupils. There were houses and gardens on either side of the road.

"Carol? She's the only one I can think of but she's cross with me."

"Your friend? No, Mum knows her mother. Have you fallen out with her?"

"Yes. Sort of. I'll have to think."

"Is everything else all right?"

She must not tell her about the row with Mum after Libby had failed to turn up that day. "I'm fine. But I was so upset, Libby…"

"I know. I'm sorry. But it's so difficult. Can you get to London?"

"London? I suppose so."

"I'd meet you. At Victoria. It takes only about thirty-five minutes."

"On the train? Libby, I haven't got much money,

only what's left of the ten shillings you left me on the dressing table. I started spending it."

"You've still got some left? After all this time? Yes, on the train. I can give you money for your fare."

"Do you live in London?"

"I'll tell all then. You haven't said a word to anyone?"

"No." She was glad to be able to say that. She had been tempted to tell Carol everything and it was only Carol, by her rejection, who had stopped her.

"It's holidays soon, isn't it? I'm sure that will make it easier. What about –let me see—Thursday week?"

"I can tell Mum I'm seeing a friend from school though I don't like telling lies. What time?"

"Yes, I know and I'm sorry. But it's Mum's attitude that has put us in this situation. What about midday? Twelve o'clock. Trains are two an hour, a quarter to and a quarter past. The journey is thirty-five minutes. Look, here's your fare. Keep it safe." Libby reached into her handbag to pull out two one pound notes.

"That's a lot," Mattie said. She tucked the notes into her satchel.

"Look, I'm going down this road. I've got to get to the station. I need to catch the quarter past four. I'm so worried about being seen. Think up a way I can write to you."

"I will."

"How's school?"

"Fine. Oh, no! Absolutely lovely. I came top in French, in the year and in exams and high up in most other subjects, except maths."

They come to a road junction. And Libby had stopped walking.

"Are you going now?"

"I must. For lots of reasons, one being I don't want you in trouble."

Would it be that much trouble if word reached Mum that she had been seen with Libby? What on earth was it all about? She would have to wait nearly two weeks before finding out. Such a long time.

Libby kissed her goodbye and was off at a fast pace. At least Mattie knew now that she was in London. London was a big place, somewhere she did not often visit. The thought of travelling up there on her own was daunting but she would do it to see Libby.

CHAPTER FOUR

A big lie and a big adventure—Mattie was not sure she could cope.

"Where are you going?" Mum asked her as she prepared to leave the house.

"To see my friends."

"Where?"

"I dunno. Not till we've met up. Around, you know."

"I don't know. What time will you be back?"

"Not late. Well before tea-time."

Mum was not satisfied with that. Mattie, not waiting to find out how dissatisfied her mother was, slipped out of the back door and along the back entry. She hurried in the direction of the railway station but it could have been anywhere. Honeyhill Street was towards the western edge of the town.

In her handbag, which seemed small and childish to her now, as well as money and a handkerchief, were poems and drawings for Libby, including the copies she had made of the ones she had thought had been sent to her.

'Is it bad to tell a lie
For a good reason?
How good does a reason
Have to be
To be good enough?
How will I know?'

The drawing beneath this one depicted a person, bent with shame, creeping out of a door.

'Are wise owls always old?
Or can you be wise
When you are young,
And can you be silly
When you are old?'

To reach the railway station, she needed to cross the town. The walk took her half an hour. Her ticket, a cheap day return, she purchased easily enough, and found the platform for the London bound train. But when it drew into the station, panic seized her. The engine was noisy, the announcements unclear. How could she be sure it was the right train and that she had not made some stupid mistake in her enquiries?

Really alarmed now, she glanced around her.

"Hi! Matt!"

Standing not more than a few yards away, about to board the train, was Lola Johnson. Usually, Lola would have been among the last of the people she would have wanted to see, but today, she was a gift.

"Lola!"

"Watch'er. Going to London? So are we." In pencil skirt and high-heels, and tugging the hand of an older version of herself, Lola moved over to Mattie. She pulled open the compartment door. Relieved, Mattie clambered in. Lola and her companion followed.

"I don't like these compartments," Mattie said as if she travelled regularly.

"Yeah, I know. No corridor. Shouldn't be allowed. My Mum's always warning me. We're going to Battersea, to the fun fair. This is my sister, Nina."

Mattie smiled at Nina. She seemed quiet. That was good. Coping with two Lolas would have been difficult.

"Where you going?" Lola spoke in phrases, not sentences. It was not surprising that she was not very good at English.

"To see a relative."

Lola expressed her opinion. "Boring," she said with a mock scowl.

"Not this one," Mattie said and that was the tenor of the conversation for the next half hour, Lola not being serious about anything.

Mattie made sure that Lola and Nina alighted first in case Libby was visible. As she stepped down onto the platform, she glanced towards the ticket barrier. Libby was there. No waiting and worrying this time. Lola and Nina were in a hurry and Lola waved as she and her sister pushed through the people ahead of them. Mattie held back, still not wanting to be seen with Libby. She fiddled with her handbag as though looking for her ticket, which she already had in her hand. Once Lola and Nina had been swallowed up by the crowds, Mattie hurried towards Libby, waving.

"Oh, it's good to see you," she said, throwing herself at Libby for a hug.

"It's worked," Libby said, smiling. She looked better than when Mattie had first seen her outside the school gates some weeks ago. "Everything good?"

"Well, apart from telling Mum a lie, yes. I said I was seeing friends from school. It was lucky, I saw one school friend on the train, so it was true."

Libby smiled, gazing at her as if to make up for the long months in which she had not seen her. "I'm so

67

happy to see you. Shall we have a snack lunch?"

Mattie allowed her sister to guide her out of the station, along a noisy road. Outside a small cafe, Libby paused. "In here. It's far enough away from the station, in case anyone else from Sittendon is coming up to London for the day."

Libby chose a small round table in a corner. For herself, she ordered coffee and a cheese roll. For Mattie, after some deliberation, a lemonade and a cheese roll. Mattie gave a little wriggle of delight.

"This is super, isn't it?" She bit into her roll. "Now tell me where you live."

"In Greenwich. Not far from where a V2 rocket landed. It's still a bit of a mess round there."

"And what are you doing?" Mattie didn't want to think about V2 rockets and the war. She could remember how afraid she had been then.

"I'm looking after someone. A lady."

"I see." These were the easy questions. "I want to know why you left."

"If I tell you, it might all slip out and I don't want that to happen."

"You mean, I'd let you down?"

"No. I'm going to keep quiet about it all for the time being, because there are so many complications, so many people to be hurt, including you."

"You'd never hurt me, would you?"

"I wouldn't, not any more than I have done and it wasn't my choice, then. It's best as it is. For a while. Believe me."

Mattie, about to take a second bite of her role, gave Libby a long, hard look. She narrowed eyes to look shrewd. "It's Mum, isn't it?"

Libby actually laughed. "Stop trying to look all-knowing. I'll give you my address if you promise not to come and find me." She reached into her handbag and passed a piece of paper over to Mattie.

"Gosh, thanks. Where's that? Greenwich?"

"Near to Greenwich."

Mattie felt in her own handbag. She carefully pulled out the pictures and poems she'd brought for Libby whose eyes filled with tears as she read them.

"They're lovely, Mattie, they're lovely. I'll keep them, carefully. For ever and ever."

This was unexpected. Now she wanted to cry, too. The poems and pictures were supposed to make her sister laugh, or at least, smile.

"Have you thought about how I could contact you?"

"Oh, only not Carol." Mattie's voice was all but a groan. "She's gone off me. She's at the Secondary Modern. She's had her hair permed, she wears high heels and she's going to work in Woolworth's on Saturdays."

"Things change, don't they, Mattie."

"Too much. I first needed to see you because I was upset because Carol didn't want me to go to the Grammar School. I tried so hard to keep friends with her. I just talked to her about you in their garden shed, sitting on the floor. I couldn't mention you at home. Mum goes potty if I do."

Libby's coffee cup wobbled as she replaced it in the saucer. Her eyes became wet again. "Oh, Mattie, has Mum been awful?"

"Not too bad. She's bothered about me being at the Grammar."

"You mean Mum? Or Carol?"

69

"Both. Mum comes out with nasty remarks and yet she shows off about me to Aunt Delia. And to Veronica Fitzgerald's Mum."

"Is Veronica at the Grammar School?"

"No, she failed. She's gone to some private school."

"And Carol?"

"She was friends with me until I let her down that Saturday I was supposed to meet you in Ammerfield. I forgot about her, I was so excited about seeing you."

"And then I didn't turn up. I'm so sorry. I really am upset. How awful."

"You see, I needed to talk to you about her, then I needed to talk to her about you. Silly, really."

After that, Libby plied her with questions about Mum, Dad, the boys, school. She replied, elaborating on the Grammar School experience, describing Drusilla Parkinson, a show-off and the form chatterbox, Barbara with her ambitious mother, Rosemary, who was warm, ordinary and quiet and as bemused as she was herself about some aspects of the Grammar School. Mattie entertained Libby and was overjoyed to see and hear her laughing at her description of the lovely Mr Shepherd, the teachers nicknamed Taffy, but left out the bit about truanting. Before she knew it, an hour had passed, Libby said it was time to go. They made promises to meet again just like today, in exactly four weeks' time.

"I'll come to the train with you to see you on safely," Libby said. She had gone all quiet and serious. She found Mattie a compartment with two ladies already sitting in there, which made Mattie feel safe. When she reached home, instead of demanding to know where she had been her mother was waiting with a message for her.

"You must be very popular at that school," was how Mum greeted her.

"What d'you mean?" Mattie feared what might follow this.

"Your friend came around."

"My friend?"

"Rosemary."

"Oh, Rosemary!" Relief and pleasure mixed to lighten her mood.

"Yes. Rosemary. Milton Stanwick. She wants you to go to tea, on Monday. So I said you could. I liked her. She'll meet you off the bus, two o'clock from the bus station. The Ammerfield bus. Ask for the church, she said."

* * *

Mum wanted Mattie to dress up to go the tea at Rosemary's.

"You mean that babyish, so-called best dress?" Mattie said with scorn. "No, I'll wear my old comfy dress and my sandals." The sandals were this year's school sandals, brown, plain and already well-scuffed. She could never make them last more than one season. Besides, although she didn't know much about Rosemary's home life, except that she was an only child and the house was small, she realised that it was in the country and there would be dust and dirt.

Rosemary was waiting at Milton Stanwick church. She wore dungarees so Mattie knew the decision she'd made about clothes was the right one.

"It's so quiet," she said, alighting just as the church clock struck half-past two. Both girls rolled around with laughter. "I wish I lived in the country."

They walked along the side of the road, Mattie observing thick hedgerows and horse chestnut and beech trees crowding the outskirts of the village. Rosemary led her down a lane off the main road. Soon, they arrived at a row of flint cottages.

"Ours is the end one," Rosemary opened a gate into a garden of riotous colour, from cornflowers, poppies and marigolds.

"Round the back," Rosemary said and there were more flowers as well as vegetables, runner beans growing up canes, a pen of chickens, and two cats slinking along the fence. A dog barked. Swallows swooped overhead.

Enchanted, Mattie paused. "Isn't it lovely?"

"It's small," Rosemary said.

"Hello, Rosie, is this your friend from school?"

Mattie turned at the voice. It was a smart voice, a bit like Barbara Ellington's Mummy's voice. Mattie hadn't expected that.

"You must be Martha," Mrs Hadlow went on. She held out her hand. It was grubby. When Mattie took it, it felt hard and dry.

"Yes, hallo, Mrs Hadlow."

Mrs Hadlow gave a little laugh. "Come on in and have a glass of lemonade. You'll need it on a warm day like this."

Mattie entered the tiny cottage. The kitchen was small. There was a range, a bit like the one in Honeyhill Street, but more modern and well black-leaded. A kitchen cabinet had its enamel tray down on which stood two glasses and a jug of lemonade. There was a small table with chairs under the window. Lots of things were hanging, herbs, dried flowers. While drinking her lemonade, Mattie took the chance to look at Mrs Hadlow. She was unexpected, a large, hefty woman, but not fat, with short hair. She wore a shirt with trousers tucked into huge socks and muddy boots.

"Come upstairs and see my room," Rosemary said leading the way from the kitchen straight into a sitting-room with a brick fireplace. Narrow stairs curved up to a small landing with three doors.

"That's Mum's room," Rosemary said, indicating a half open door beyond which was an unmade bed. "That's the bathroom. Hardly room to swing a bath towel, Mum says. This is mine."

Rosemary's room was also small, being above half the kitchen and overlooking the spilling, pretty garden and those of the neighbours, which were not so carefully cultivated. There was space for only a single bed, a chest of drawers and a bookcase.

"I didn't know it was this small, your house," Mattie said. Small was relative. When Rosemary had said her house was small, Mattie had thought that Rosemary had meant compared to Barbara Ellington's house, also in Milton Stanwick, much talked about by Barbara. But this was truly small.

"I'll take you down to the garden in a minute. We can go and look for eggs."

"Eggs?"

"Hens'. For tea."

"How do you fit three people into such a small house?"

"Three?"

"Your Dad?"

"I don't have, one. He died. In the war. There's just me and Mum. Mum works on the farm, Datchmore's

73

farm. She's a dairy maid." Rosemary giggled. "She looks after the cows. She milks them."

"Really? Do women do that?"

Rosemary shrugged. "They did during the war. She was a land girl."

"It's all so small," Mattie couldn't help saying again and again.

"Well, we're not rich. I have to have a grant for my uniform. We couldn't afford it, otherwise."

Mattie had always understood that Rosemary's family was not in the same league of wealth as Barbara Ellington's, but that anyone could be poor with that voice she could not understand. Despite the voice though, she felt comfortable with Rosemary's mother in the modest home. She would have no hesitation in inviting Rosemary to tea at her own home later in the holiday. Mum would have to put up with her imaginings about her Grammar School friends.

The afternoon flew by, as pleasant afternoons always did. Mattie played with one of the cat's adorable kittens, wishing she dared ask Mum if she could have one. With Rosemary, she looked for eggs in the chicken run. Mrs Hadlow had left them there that morning so Mattie could search for them. For tea, it was those eggs, boiled, bread and butter, home-made jam, and jelly and bottled raspberries from the garden.

"Do you like it at the Grammar School?" Mrs Hadlow asked over tea.

Mattie hesitated. "Yes, on the whole. Algebra worries me."

"Oh," Mrs Hadlow laughed. "Algebra. It used to worry me."

"Did you go to the Grammar School?"

"Oh, no. It wasn't like it is now. It's easier since those days. If Rosie was not at the Grammar School, if things had not changed, she would be leaving in two years time. In those days, if you went to Elementary school, you left at fourteen."

"Mum ran away from boarding school," Rosemary said. "She was twelve, weren't you, Mum?"

"I didn't appreciate education," Mrs Hadlow said, "otherwise I would have got my matriculation and be doing something else besides milking cows. I have high hopes for Rosie."

* * *

Preparing Mum to ask her to allow Rosemary's invitation to tea to be returned was more of a problem.

"I think," Mattie said tactfully, "it would be polite if I asked Rosemary to come here to tea," she ventured one afternoon.

Mum sniffed, looked away and said, "We'll see."

Mattie tried again, days later. "You remember I was telling you about Rosemary?"

"One of your friends at school?"

"Yes, that's right. The one who came here. The one I went to tea with. You said you liked her."

"Where did you say she lived? Was it Gracehill? Because I don't want anyone from there, coming sniffing round here and reporting back to the Fitzgeralds."

"No, not Gracehill. Milton Stanwick."

"Same thing," Mum said. "They all know each other."

"No, Rosemary's mother is not like that. She's really nice. She works on a farm."

"Oh, yes. Doing the accounts, is that it? I never

75

knew a poor farmer. They've all got loads of money. Even these days."

"You've got the wrong idea."

"Huh? Not again, surely. Look, Mattie, I don't want your Grammar School friends here. If I'd known it was going to be like this..."

"I know. You'd have sent me to the Sec Mod. I'd have been miserable there with everyone being jealous of me because I'm clever."

"You think so, do you? You think you're clever?"

"Well, I am. That's how I got to the Grammar School. And it's not a bit comfortable for me, with you more worried about what people think of you than what I think of you." Mattie burst into tears and ran up the two flights of narrow stairs to her bedroom, stumbling on the second flight.

Mum came up to see if she was hurt.

"Oh, I suppose I'll have to let this girl come here," she said, seeing Mattie was only suffering from a slight bruise. "That'll go down if you come downstairs and I'll put a cold compress on it."

Mattie wanted to say she'd already put a cold compress on her heart, but refrained. There was no point in retaining her anger in victory.

So, Rosemary came to tea at the end of August. Mum was all of a dither. She laid out tea, on the best table cloth, in the kitchen. Money she could not afford she spent on cakes, scones, meat and fish pastes for sandwiches, chocolate biscuits and lemonade. She adopted her best voice and fussed over Rosemary. All morning she had been cleaning and polishing. Mattie was embarrassed and said so afterwards, pointing out that Rosemary had had just one salmon paste sandwich, one scone with butter and no jam and one slender slice of Victoria sponge. Mum accused Mattie of being ungrateful.

* * *

The second visit to Libby was made in August, just before the beginning of the Autumn term. These trips to London were to follow the pattern of the first trip, going to the same cafe, having the same rolls, telling each other the same news. Each time, Mattie gave Mum the same explanation.

"I'm going out with my friends from school. I'll be home in time for tea."

"Who are they?" Mum asked on the third occasion.

"Oh, girls from Gracehill."

Mattie knew that would dry up any further questions.

SECOND YEAR
1951-52

CHAPTER FIVE

Autumn term started in early September. Mattie and her friends were now Second Years, still with Mr Shepherd as form master. Her form was 2B. The intake of First Years appeared to be small and young, overwhelmed by their new, large uniforms.

Mattie's own school uniform, when she put it on for the first day of term, had either shrunk or she had grown, both up and out. She said nothing to Mum, anticipating a grumble about the expense of the Grammar School and how humiliating it had been having to apply for a grant a year ago.

The maths teacher, Mr Watts, spoke to Mattie to see how he could help with her problems with algebra. He was kind, promising to help her by setting special, easier questions to work on at home that would, he hoped, gradually improve her understanding and her confidence.

"I've decided," she told Rosemary, "I'm not the mathematical type. I'm more English and French."

On the morning, during the half-term break in October, she was preparing for her trip to London to meet Libby, a letter arrived that sent the Dobson household into a frenzy. Mum opened it, her face white, her fingers trembling. Mattie, Frank and Tony knew the contents must be momentous.

Mum sat down at the kitchen table. She read it and became all fluttery and had to lean her head on her hands.

"What is it?" Mattie said, suspending her anxiety to leave and catch the train.

Mum sat up. Her forehead was damp. But she was smiling.

"I'll have to try to find your father," she said, and her voice shook. "Is he in the parks today, or the cemetery?"

"Why?" Mattie said.

"We've been allocated a council house," Mum said as the letter slipped from her nervous hand.

Tony was on his knees to grasp it. Mattie held out her hand for it.

"Where? When?" Frank said.

"Hill Common," Mum said, taking the letter from Mattie before she could see anything on it. "Oakfield Road, wherever that is. It's new. Three bedrooms. Me and Dad, we've got to go and see it Tuesday and to sign up for it. It's not quite ready yet. Your Grandma lived there, Hill Common."

The stunned silence that followed was broken only by the cheers from Frank and Tony.

"Oakfield Road," Mattie said. "That's quite close to my school. At the back, by the back gates."

She was anxious to leave to catch the train. The conversation with Rosemary and Conor in the park, on the day they had played truant, came to her mind.

"*Is there something wrong with Hill Common?*" Rosemary had asked and Conor had replied that it was a council estate. Well, of course it was, it was full of council houses, new council houses, and the Dobsons were going to live in one. There was nothing wrong with it. She could hardly wait to tell Libby.

* * *

"We're going to move," Mattie greeted Libby, who was waiting in her usual place by the ticket barrier.

"Move?"

"Yes, a letter came this morning. We're moving to Hill Common. The new estate."

"Oh, how lovely." Libby sounded pleased, but watching her face, Mattie was not convinced. There was a cloud, a reservation in the words. Libby knew she was never going to live in the new house.

On this occasion, Mattie chose a spam roll and a cup of tea, just for a change. She wanted to remember each of these meetings with Libby and there was a possibility that they would all blur together in her memory. They were too important for her to allow that to happen.

"Write to me and tell me all about it," Libby said. "It will be getting on for Christmas before I see you again, the end of October. I need to feel I know where you are. Tell me the address, won't you?"

"Of course, but Libby, I'm running out of money. I thought of sneaking a half-crown from Mum's purse this morning..."

"Don't do that, please. Never do anything like that. She'd spot it."

Mattie promised and Libby handed her another two pound notes. "You see, I've been buying 'Girls' Crystal' every week and I swap it with Lola Johnson for her 'School Friend'."

* * *

After the October visit, the preparations for the move, the packing, the dreaming, the window shopping for unaffordable items, overshadowed Mattie's planning for the Christmas party. This was to be in the last week of term and this year, Mattie would be able to go. She prayed for a new dress, she prayed for a pink and blue bedroom and she prayed for Libby. Algebra-anxiety was relegated to the back of her mind.

The family went to see the house after Mum and Dad had signed for it.

"It's beautiful," Mattie said as she stood in the muddy Oakfield Road before her new home.

"Isn't it?" Mum said happily. She had been shown over it by someone from the council

"Home," Dad murmured.

The house was an ordinary house, three-bedroomed, semi-detached, in raw pink brick, but it was beautiful. Mum and Dad had obtained the key to it after paying rent one week in advance. The front garden was a mound of clay. The family stood gazing at it.

"Can we go in, Mum?"

Mum took the keys from her handbag. She gazed at them in her hand as though they were the Crown Jewels. Her face, Mattie noticed, had been become soft-looking.

"Yes," Mum said, "we can go in. Try not to tread in the mud. That could be difficult because it's all over the path."

Mattie and Dad followed her along the path, picking their way round the clods of earth. The boys followed them. Mum put the key in the lock, turned it and pushed the door to reveal the hall and staircase of their new home. Everyone trooped in, no one spoke. The boys managed to find a lot of mud to take in with them. The floors downstairs were a shiny brown colour.

"Poured floors," Mum said. "I was told not to drop things, they break. So be careful."

Mattie heaved a happy sigh as Dad closed the front door behind them. The place smelled of new wood. She thought of Libby, never going to live here.

"Home," Dad muttered again.

"This is the sitting room," Mum said, opening the door to the right. The room had a big picture window overlooking the mud of the front garden-to-be and similar, but unfinished, houses on the opposite side of the road. A fireplace, with doors on it, faced the window.

"It heats the water," Mum said. "Imagine, hot water."

Mattie imagined. A bath? How luxurious!

Mum led the way back through the hall to the kitchen-diner.

"We'll eat here," she said. "I'll have to buy an electric cooker. No gas, you see. I don't know anything about electric cookers. Are they dear?"

"HP," Dad murmured. "From the Electricity Board."

"And curtains. I'll have to get curtains."

Mattie wanted to see her bedroom. She followed Mum up the naked wooden staircase. There were three bedrooms. Frank and Tony would have the second bedroom overlooking the back garden, mounds of clay at the moment. Mattie was to have the little room at the side, all to herself for the first time. Again, she thought of Libby. Nobody mentioned her not seeing the new house. The small room looked out over the mud-mound of a front garden and the path up to the house next door, the one which was not attached.

Gazing out the window of the boys' bedroom, she could see that the semi -attached house next door was on a corner. An old lane led up the hill. At the top, just out of her vision, obscured by the lane's hedges, were the back gates of the Grammar School. Directly below the window, a bank with steps led from the back door up to the would-be garden.

"A rockery," Dad murmured, gazing enraptured at the bank. Mattie thought of Rosemary's mother's garden in Milton Stanwick, and of Carol's father's garden with its shed. Perhaps Dad would make something of this mound of clay.

The bathroom had a toilet, a bath and a hand basin. The light was operated by a pull cord.

"So modern," Mattie said, eyeing the bath. She had never, in her memory, lived in a house with a bath. To think of ending the embarrassing sessions in the kitchen, with the baby bath, water boiled in the kettle and added to cold water, and the door locked to keep out the rest of the family, would be bliss, freedom. She would now be like the other girls at school who spoke of bath salts and washing their hair in the hand basin.

"Fancy us having an indoor toilet," Mum said.

"There's another one, out the back," Dad said. "Two toilets, we've arrived."

"When do we move in, Mum?"

"End of November."

Mattie's heart did a dive. This was about the time she was to see Libby, after the next visit. She would have to let her know once the date was fixed. It was also too close to the Christmas party. All attention would be diverted to the move, the buying of the electric cooker, new curtains. Mum would be in her element. She would have no time for party dresses and no money, either. Silence was best maintained on this issue. She would wear the dress she had been meant to wear last year if she could get into it. It would be wrong to bother Mum about such a triviality.

But such restraint was impossible and she found herself dropping the occasional heavy, guilt–laden hint.

* * *

In preparation for the move, Mattie carefully packed her belongings. As well as Libby's schoolgirl stories, there were books of her own, some of which were childish and could be sent to a jumble sale. She had a box of her drawings and poems, especially the ones for Libby, poems which were supposed to be secret, so she tied the lid on with string. Some of her clothes could go to the jumble sale, too. She was too old for dresses with puffed sleeves.

The move was accomplished while she was at school one day in November, after her half-term visit to Libby, sooner than Mum had predicted. For the last time, Mattie left Honeyhill Street for school and went home, for the first time, to Oakfield Road, through the back gates of the Grammar School.

Approaching the house, number sixty-four (only one higher!) there was no sign from the outside of the predicted upheaval.

"I'll never find anything," Mum had kept saying as tea chest after tea chest was filled.

Dad had the day off. Mattie knocked on the front door.

"Come round the back," Mum's voice shouted from somewhere inside the house.

"Come round the back," Dad's quieter and calmer

voice came from the side of the house where a door led to the back. He was standing there, holding it open.

"Is it nice?" Mattie bounced up to him. "Do you like it?"

"It's splendid," he said.

Inside was chaos and a panicking Mum.

"D'you want a cup of tea? D'you want a cup of tea?" Mum kept saying

"I think your Mum wants a cup of tea," Dad said, lifting the new electric kettle to the tap. He plugged it in and switched it on. He and Mattie stood watching and waiting for it to boil. "Electricity Board," he added, pointing to the kettle.

Mum appeared, all fluttery. "D'you want a cup of tea?" she said.

"On its way," Dad said.

The boys came round the back and burst in with gasps of wonderment, whether it was about the house or about the chaos, it was difficult to tell.

"Blimey," Frank said. "Boxes everywhere."

"Up to your room," Mum said. "And stay there. It's bad enough without you two making it worse."

"Aw!" Tony pouted.

"Take your shoes off first," Mum shouted as they were about to leave the kitchen.

Mattie poured a cup of tea from the teapot that Dad had filled from the electric kettle. She told Mum to go into the sitting room and she'd bring the tea into her. It was almost as though Mum wanted to be told what to do,

Mattie went up to her room. Boxes with her name on them were in there, with her bed, Libby's book case and her own chest of drawers. A big bundle of her bedclothes squatted in the middle of the muddle. She untied it and set about making up the bed. Sitting on the edge of the made bed, she surveyed her new, private sanctuary. The familiar knitted-squares bedspread, made by Grandma, was comfortingly familiar. She would be quite happy here, doing her homework.

* * *

"I expect my party dress from last year will still fit," she murmured, over her porage one breakfast during their first week at Oakfield Road. "Though I wouldn't know where on earth to find it."

No one responded. She hadn't expected a response. Life was chaotic, with the unfamiliarity of the new house, so many things still unpacked. She tried to forget about the party but that was not easy. At school it was the only topic of conversation.

Lola Johnson – it had to be Lola Johnson – brought up the subject when their journeys to school coincided. Mattie recalled that this girl lived on Hill Common, too.

"I'm getting my party dress after school today," Lola said before she had even caught up with Mattie. She was a tall girl, quick in her movements and deadly on the hockey field. "My Mum is taking me shopping after school. I'm getting shoes as well. There'll be more dancing this year. Last year it was all games, wasn't it?"

"I couldn't be there last year," Mattie said. She almost wished she wouldn't be there again this year.

"Oh, yeah. Your Nan died, didn't she? I wouldn't have cared if that had been me."

"I wasn't allowed."

"Blimey. What killjoys your lot are. I wish the

89

dancing we've been taught in PT was ballroom. Square dancing and country dancing, it's a bit childish, isn't it?"

Mattie agreed. You didn't disagree with Lola. Whether she was to be feared more than Drusilla and Barbara, was difficult to decide. Lola Johnson was their exact opposite and posed fears of other kinds of humiliation.

Not long before the party, Mattie arrived home, a blood red sun sinking on the horizon, frost in the air, her finger tips tingling from the cold.

"On your bed," Mum said as Mattie brought in a blast of cold air.

"What's on my bed?"

"Shut that door, quickly. Go up and see."

Mattie kicked off her shoes in the hall, poked her feet into her slippers and hurried up to the bedroom. Spread out on her bed was a dress, a cream-coloured broderie anglais dress in the 'new look' style of a couple of years back. It had a long flared skirt, cap sleeves and tiny revere collars. It would make her waist look slim. She slung off her coat and school uniform to try on the dress. She ran down the stairs, lifting the skirt, to Mum. Only one flight of stairs here.

"It's lovely! Thanks, Mum." She ran up to her mother to kiss her. "Where did you get it? It's lovely."

Mum brushed off the gratitude, although she was clearly pleased. "WVS," she muttered. "It's not new, of course."

"New to me. I love it."

"It's a bit long for you. I'll see if I can shorten it for you. Did you see the shoes?"

"Shoes as well?"

She flew back up the stairs to find a pair of low

heeled court shoes in red, also from the WVS. She was not sure she would have preferred the silver sandals from last year, but such goodwill from Mum was enough motivation to wear them and perhaps even Lola Johnson would admire red court shoes.

There would be a lot of news to tell Libby on the next visit, just after the Second Years' Christmas Party.

CHAPTER SIX

The 'Girls' Crystal Annual', a Christmas present from Libby, had needed to be hidden until after the last day of term when its presence in her room could be explained as a present from a school friend.

At the stroke of midnight, the second the New Year began, there was a knock on the front door. Mum answered it. It was Barry Wood, from next door. He came in with a piece of coal, 'First Footing.' Mum and Mrs Wood, his mother, had agreed this. "For luck", Mum explained, "an old tradition in some parts of the country."

The whole Dobson family then trooped round to next door for drinks, which was only cider. The house, number sixty two, was attached to number sixty-four. Mr Woods, senior, was a caretaker at a small primary school. Mrs Woods had Barry, Pauline and Dorothy. Pauline went to the secondary modern school and was older than Mattie. Dorothy was only eight.

"You go to the Grammar?" Pauline said, wide-eyed.

"Yes."

"You're clever, then?"

"Not really. Do you know Carol Millington at your school?"

"No, I don't think I do. What year?"

"Second."

"Oh, I'm fourth. I leave next year, I mean this year, in the summer."

Frank and Tony were talking to Barry, who was tall

and dark, a bit shy and sixteen. He was loving the attention from the boys. Mattie did not realise at first that he kept glancing at her. Mum had noticed though, and her lips were pressed into the hard line. After the little chatty party, the Dobsons returned home. Frank and Tony tumbled to their room. They had never been allowed up so late. Mattie was glad to fall into her bed in her little room.

"This year," Mum said to Mattie when she went down to breakfast next morning, "is going to be interesting. Fidelma, Delia told me yesterday afternoon, is getting married before Easter."

Mattie looked up eagerly from her porage. Instead of drawing owls, as she had planned for this morning, she might try sketching a wedding dress for Fidelma.

"Oh, that's great." Mattie said.

"You think so?" Mum said.

"Of course I do. Is she going to ask me to be bridesmaid?"

"Yes. She is."

"Oh, goody. I've never been a bridesmaid."

Mum's mouth was in the straight line Mattie dreaded. What now? It was difficult to think of a reason.

"And Frank is sitting the scholarship in February," Mum said. She sounded less grim about that than she had about Fidelma's wedding.

"Is he going to the Christian Brothers'?"

"No. Your Dad refuses to allow it. If he passes, which I very much doubt, he will go to your school."

"My school? Oh, I'm not sure about that."

"Don't be so selfish," Mum said. "He is as likely to get in as you were."

She had not meant that at all. She had been thinking of Frank telling tales on her. Not that she planned to be in trouble, of course, but if algebra got too difficult she might play truant again. Breaking rules was always easier if you had already done it once, like the visits to Libby. The plan was for another visit to her in the middle of January. Mattie paid intense attention to the weather forecasts on the wireless, fearing that heavy snow might spoil the plans.

The day Frank sat his written exam for the Eleven-Plus, as it was now called, an extraordinary event occurred. Form 2B were in the Geography room, learning about rocks of ages. One boy, Robin Chester, from a farm in Milton Stanwick, put up his hand. He was a sort of unofficial spokesman for the form.

"Yes, Chester," the Geography teacher, Mr Jones said.

"Please, sir, why is the flag at half-mast?" The whole form turned to gaze at the flag over the playing fields. It was indeed at half-mast.

"Well observed, Chester, though I would have preferred it if your attention was focused on my lesson. However, on this occasion, I will overlook it. The flag is at half-mast because the King has died."

There was a silence, then one or two giggles as if some people thought Mr Jones was joking.

"Really?" a few voices asked.

"Yes. Peacefully. In his sleep."

"Oh! What happens? Do we get to go home? Who's King now?" A clamour of voices besieged Mr Jones.

"We have a new monarch. Presumably Queen Elizabeth. She is in Kenya but coming home. There will be a Royal Funeral."

"She'll have to be coronated, won't she, sir, Princess Elizabeth?"

"I think you mean crowned, Jasper. Yes, there will be a coronation."

Mattie thought it dreadful that the King had died the very day Frank was taking his exam. She hoped it wouldn't make a difference.

Later that day Drusilla made contact with Mattie. They spoke only occasionally these days and had hardly exchanged a word this Spring term.

"I've been wanting to ask you," Drusilla said as their paths crossed on the way to the canteen for lunch. "Is it right you live on Hill Common, now?"

She gazed at Mattie with big, innocent eyes full of amusement.

"Yes. It is right. I do."

"Really? A council estate? Are you anywhere near Lola Johnson?"

Too near, if the truth were to be told. But Mattie chose to lie about this. "I don't really know," she said. "Why, are you friends with her now?"

"No. But I thought you might be."

Drusilla sauntered away. Rosemary had been watching.

"You all right?" she said to Mattie

"Yes." Mattie linked arms with Rosemary. "But she's not. She's unkind. She's having a go because I live in a council estate now."

"You shouldn't have told anyone."

"Can't avoid it. She comes to school through the back gate. Everyone who comes that way knows because my house is right by the lane near the gate. I didn't know people looked down on council estates."

"Well, don't worry, we've got an extra day off next

95

week for the funeral. Will you watch it on TV?"

"We haven't got one," Mattie said, glum. She was beginning to feel she could not live up to the expectations of the Grammar School. And anyway why should she not tell anyone where she lived? She wasn't ashamed to live on a council estate.

When she reached home, her mother was out the back, talking over the chain-link fencing to Mrs Wood next door. Mattie saw a slim book cross the fence as Mrs Wood passed it to Mum. It wasn't a magazine. It was smaller than that and anyway, Mum didn't believe in wasting time reading magazines. Perhaps she was reading books now. Perhaps she felt better, living in the house at Oakfield Road. It was easier to keep clean, not so many stairs and it was certainly warmer. The book was tucked into the pocket of Mum's flowered pinafore and Mattie forgot about it.

* * *

Mrs Wood invited the Dobsons to watch the King's funeral on the Woods' television. How everyone was going to fit in, ten people altogether, and for a long while, was a mystery.

She did it, though. Their children sat on the floor, Mr and Mrs Wood had the dining chairs, Mum and Dad were on the sofa, Mattie had one of the armchairs and the boys squashed themselves together in the other one. Barry was on the floor next to Mattie's chair. He shared a packet of Smiths' crisps with her.

"Bring hankies," Mrs Wood had said and she was wise to think of it. There was a lot of sniffling and snuffling because it was sad.

At home, talk about Frank and the scholarship dominated the household. Mattie's anger about it surprised her. It wasn't fair. Her next visit to Libby, for her birthday, was taken up with this topic.

"They, Mum and Dad, never talked about me going to the Grammar School like they're talking about Frank," she said. "It's, Frank, if you do this, you'll be able to do that. If you get to the Grammar School, on and on it goes."

"They didn't expect you to pass," Libby said.

"I don't know why not."

"He's a boy. They believe it matters for him."

"Yeah, I know. 'I don't want him to end up in Parks and Gardens like me,' Dad said. When I said, 'Oh, it would be okay for me to be a skivvy, is that right?' they got cross. 'Mattie, you're becoming very argumentative since you've been at that Grammar School,' Mum said."

Libby laughed. She was not surprised by any of this. "They worry, about all of us."

"Not about you."

"Yes, they do."

"Well, I said, 'Let's hope Frank has failed. You don't want him being argumentative, too.' After that, I grabbed my satchel and ran out of the back door. Did I tell you Fidelma's getting married?"

"No, you did not. How long have you known?"

"Since the New Year. What do you do all day, Libby?"

"Some days, I do a bit of hairdressing. To bring in some money, you know? And, as you know, I look after someone, a lady. She's old and not very well."

"Where do you live? How would I get there?"

"Mattie, you must not visit until I tell you. Please."

* * *

Fidelma's wedding took place just before Easter.

"Father Tully doesn't like to solemnise marriage during Lent," Mum said darkly to Delia.

"Can't be helped," Delia said.

The guests were the same people as the mourners at Grandma's funeral, only more brightly dressed. Mum wore her best 'new look' dress which she'd had since 1949. It was long, and needed high heels. She had her hair done and even looked pretty, mostly because she was enjoying herself. There was laughter, they sang and danced, like at the funeral. They drank even more. The only difference was that the church bit was over and done with at the beginning. The uncles got drunk, and were thrown out by Mum and Delia. Mattie had an apple green satin dress as a bridesmaid which Frank spoiled by spilling Guinness on it.

Some days after the wedding, Mum said casually, "Did anyone tell you Fidelma is expecting a baby?".

"No. She's not, is she? Already?" Mattie said.

"Yes. I have a little book for you."

"For my birthday? It's not till April."

"No, for your life. Here." Mum thrust the book at her. The gesture was almost hostile. It was the book Mattie had seen being passed over the garden fence. "Read it in your bedroom."

"In my bedroom?"

"Yes. It's about growing up and things. You don't want the boys seeing it."

Mattie accepted the slender volume and took it upstairs to her room. She glanced at it with mild contempt. Biology, about human beings. She giggled. It

98

would have been impossible to have read the magazines that Libby used to share with her and still be ignorant of the topic of this book, The Facts of Life. As if, Mattie thought, she didn't know all about the Facts of Life. For a start, Libby had told her all about periods. She had told her too, about how to have a baby. It was rude, really, and embarrassing. Every time she saw a baby in a pram, Mattie marvelled at how many people seemed to do rude things and so often. Mum and Dad had done it four times. Obviously it had to be done in the dark to hide red faces. Libby and the magazines which she shared with Mattie, were full of warnings about 'going too far' and 'leading boys on', allowing them to become so excited that they had to have sexual intercourse immediately. This was the girl's responsibility, not to 'tease' the boy. What Mattie could not understand, at first, anyway, was that this thing, sexual intercourse, was painted as a temptation with enormous power and attraction. Yet the more she thought about it, the more she came to understand that it was something wonderful---but only if you were married.

CHAPTER SEVEN

Mattie's birthday was at the end of April, before term started. She had arranged with Libby to go to see her in April, instead of March. "For your birthday treat," Libby had said when they parted at the end of the previous visit. "This visit," Libby said, "will start earlier and end a bit later. Can you do it?"

" 'Course I can. April is spring. It will be lighter in the evenings. The Summer term will start shortly after that."

"So long as you're not going with boys," Mum said when she told her she might be a bit later than her usual time with her friends.

She had a wonderful day. The highlight was being taken to the pictures by Libby that afternoon. The film was called '*Limelight*', and was about a ballet dancer and an elderly clown. Mattie was captivated. She had always thought films about falling in love were 'yucky', sentimental, but she totally identified with the heroine in this film and cried copiously when the clown, whom the heroine loved, died while she was dancing on stage. This romantic notion of love was connected to sexual intercourse, she suddenly saw. Still crying, Mattie emerged into the fresh air. Libby was amused.

"It was lovely," Mattie sobbed into her handkerchief. "It was lovely. So sad. So sad. But I did enjoy it."

The film seemed to have awoken something in her. During the following weeks, she moved around the house humming the theme tune from the film and spent hours on Sunday mornings with her ear stuck to the wireless waiting for it to be requested on Family Favourites.

The summer term started and the summer uniform dress had to be tried on. It was not so big this year. A letter came to say that Frank had passed the written exam for the Grammar School and that he should attend an interview on May the twelfth at eleven o'clock. Mum didn't know whether to be proud or to worry about the cost of the uniform.

Mattie laughed. "You're not really worried about the uniform. You know about grants now. You're just worried that we're learning things you know nothing about."

Mum's reaction shocked her. "You can climb down off your high horse, madam, and apologise to me or there'll be no tea for you."

About to apologise, Mattie stopped herself. It'd been true, what she'd said. Perhaps she shouldn't have laughed. But it was true.

She turned away with a shrug.

* * *

There were rumours among the Second Year forms that the next Domestic Science lesson (and Woodwork for the boys) would be special. There was a lot of sniggering about it but no one would explain what was so special.

"They've been told not to say," Rosemary said.

"There's only a few things that people snigger about," Mattie said.

"What would they be?"

The film *'Limelight'*, that Libby had taken her to see, came to her mind. She giggled. "Falling in love," she said, "and all that."

Rosemary giggled too.

The girls of 2B filed into the Domestic Science room. They drifted to their usual seats at the deal tables, only to be told by Miss Graham, the Domestic Science teacher, to leave their places and come to the front and sit in a circle before the blackboard. Miss Graham was a busty bottle-blonde with bright lipstick. She proceeded to go into great detail about the human body, the difference between male and female, about menstruation, where babies came from and she left until last to explain how they got there. She explained about eggs (ovum,) and sperm and that they had to come together to make a baby that would grow and develop in the womb.

"Now how does the sperm get to the ovum?" she asked the class. Until now, Mattie had been totally at ease. She wore bras these days, after all. Some girls looked uncomfortable, some were pink with embarrassment. But when Lola Johnson responded to the question, calling out, "He does her, Miss."

Mattie was embarrassed for Miss Graham. There was a great gasp from the class which fell about in hysterical laughter, Mattie included.

"There are better ways of explaining sexual intercourse," poor Miss Graham said. She calmed the class. With her pointer, she indicated, on the chart that was unrolled over the blackboard, the male sexual organs, saying, "This has to put inside," and she moved the pointer to the female sexual organs, "this."

She paused, then went on hurriedly, over the sniggers, "I have to warn you, after all this frivolity, that you must not imagine you can now experiment with boys. It is dangerous. You don't want diseases and you don't want an illegitimate baby. An illegitimate baby has to be given away and adopted and that is terrible for the mother and it is terrible for the baby. People don't want to know you if you have an illegitimate baby."

Mattie stared at Miss Graham. From a minute ago, rolling about, laughing and shrieking at Lola Johnson's crude remarks, she now became frozen, as if an icy hand was gripping her heart, stopping her breath.

Miss Graham noticed that something was wrong.

"Martha, are you all right there?"

Mattie was unable to reply. A sudden flash of light had revealed a truth so awful she could not cope with it. She found herself on her feet and running from the room.

She ran down the corridor and out of a side door to the fresh air. She belted across the netball court towards the gates, which she shot out of at a speed she did not know she was capable of achieving.

After several minutes, she found herself near the gates of the park, so breathless she could run no more. Her tired legs just about carried her though the gates and over to the recreation ground. Oblivious of the possibility of encountering her father, she sat on a swing, to rock to and fro in a movement that soothed her as much as anything could.

She knew now with absolute certainty, what had happened to Libby.

* * *

103

How long she sat swinging gently she did not know. Weariness overcame her so she stretched out on the see-saw, where she dozed until disturbed by a mother and her small children. She ran off, to walk aimlessly towards the town. The Catholic Church loomed on a corner, a symbol of peace and consolation in her life, but now beginning to be a source of confusion. Inside it was cool and quiet. She settled in a pew in the darkest corner. The red sanctuary lamp flickered reassuringly. She stayed a long time. No one disturbed her. In her head, because she had no pencil, she made up a poem.

There is winter in my heart.
No light, no life, no love
Only barren ruts in the field.
Will spring ever come?

In the end, she had to go home. There was nowhere else to go.

On reaching the house, she sneaked in through the back entrance, then the kitchen door, finding no sign of Mum. She was aiming for the stairs when suddenly the sitting room door was wrenched open. Mum stood there, a wild, aggravated Mum.

"Mattie! There you are! Thank God. Where have you been?"

Mattie stared at her. She was sealed up, unable to say or do anything.

"Come in here," Mum ordered.

Mattie obeyed.

"What's the meaning of this?" Mum thrust a piece of paper under her nose.

"What is it?"

"A note. Delivered by your school secretary. You left school. In the middle of a lesson. They're worried." Mum's mouth was in a straight line.

"Libby," Mattie muttered. "I know. Sex education. Miss Graham said about illegitimate babies."

That was Mum's cue for a diatribe. She went on and on. She bellowed, she begged, she cajoled, she threatened. There was much about shame. "Everyone at the Grammar School will know now. I'll never be able to go to Parents' Evening." Through all this, Libby's name was not mentioned, Libby was not even referred to. Only Mum's distress mattered.

Mum and Dad had never been to a Parents' Evening yet. Mattie remained mute. It was no effort. Speaking would have involved effort. The boys came home from school and Mattie took herself to bed. But not to sleep. She sat up to write a plea to Libby. She found an envelope from one of her birthday cards, scratched out her name on the front of it to write Libby's address in Greenwich instead. She looked in her purse for a stamp, as Libby had given her a supply, found one, poked her feet into her school sandals before creeping downstairs and out of the back door. Nobody seemed to have heard her. Mum was busy relating to Dad what she knew of the events and expressing her anger about Mattie.

Mattie made her way across the town to the railway station where there was a post box that was cleared at nine o'clock in the evening in order to deliver the post the next morning. Mum did this sometimes if she wanted to see Aunt Delia urgently. Mattie's note had asked Libby to meet her at Victoria station tomorrow at ten o'clock. She was able to creep back indoors and up to her bedroom without being noticed.

Lulled by the low hum from downstairs as her parents discussed her and what to do about her, Mattie eventually fell asleep. She woke early the next morning and dragged herself down to breakfast.

"You all right this morning?" Mum greeted her.

"Fine." Mattie kept her eyes lowered.

"You look a bit white."

"I'm fine."

"Eat your breakfast."

"I don't want any. Just a cup of tea."

"You must have breakfast."

Mattie ignored her. She drank her tea. Frank and Tony appeared to gaze at her and clearly they were wondering what all the fuss had been about.

"I'm going," she said and ran upstairs to her room. Her satchel was on the floor beside her bed. She felt in it for her purse. When she had pulled on her cardigan, she ran down the stairs, leaving her satchel where it was. She called 'goodbye' as she slammed out of the front door.

She marched down the path, past the Woods' house next door, to turn up the lane at a furious pace. Past the school gates, against the tide of pupils surging into school, she marched, through the town to the railway station. There she asked for her usual cheap day return to London.

The train was packed with commuters, all smoking. She stood by an open window, breathing in the smuts from the engine, letting the breeze ruffle her hair. She thought of nothing. Her mind was empty. Her jaw ached from being clenched. Her eyes smarted from the smoke or wanting to cry, which it was, she neither knew nor cared.

At Victoria station, she allowed the crush to go before her and was in less of a hurry. When she looked for Libby, she saw her straightaway. At that moment her thoughts and feelings returned and she was afraid as well as angry and tearful. Libby had seen her. She was not smiling.

"Mattie! What on earth is going on?"

"You got my note?" Mattie was crying even more now.

"Yes, I did. Tell me. You look dreadful."

"Libby, I know. I know."

"Know what?" Libby's arm was round her shoulders as she led her across the concourse and out of the station. Matter felt her stiffen.

"Why you left. Can we go to the cafe? My legs are shaky. I need to sit down."

"Not in the cafe, not with you looking like that." Libby sounded almost angry. "What happened?"

"It was – school," she said between sobs. "Facts of life – you know? She said – Miss Graham did – about illegitimate babies." Mattie began to howl. Passers-by looked at her with curiosity. "How they were taken away. I can't bear it. I can't bear it."

"Hush. Please, Mattie. People are staring."

"S–sorry. S–sorry."

"Come on. I know where we can go. Somewhere quiet. Where we won't be disturbed."

"I'm – I'm already dis-disturbed." Mattie continued to sob.

Libby guided her along the pavements. She said little.

"I had to come," Mattie said.

"Ssh. Not now, Mattie. Keep moving, can you?"

"No, I'm tired."

"Not much further."

"Where are we going? It's a long way."

Libby's speed slowed. Mattie looked up. They were in some sort of square. A huge building, with stripes across it, stood before them.

"It's the Cathedral," Libby said. "Westminster Cathedral. We're going in there."

Mattie went rigid. She stopped walking. "Cathedral? If it's not a Catholic cathedral I'm not going in."

"It is."

"If you've got a priest or Father Tully there to tell me I'm a naughty girl, I'm not going in there."

"Come on, don't be silly. It'll be quiet. There'll be somewhere to sit down. People often sit crying in there, or looking upset. We'll find a quiet corner."

Nothing seemed real or safe anymore. Mattie had no choice but to trust Libby.

Inside, the Cathedral was vast. A feeling of calm and peace washed over her. The organ was playing softly. Libby led her to a quiet spot near the Lady Chapel where she sat on a chair and tugged at Mattie's hand to encourage her to do the same.

"If you come here at night, especially at Christmas, you think you're under open sky. You can't see anything above all the lights. It's beautiful. Now tell me what this is all about."

Mattie gave her sister a sidelong glance. Libby's voice sounded cross. She still wasn't smiling.

"Miss Graham, she gave us a lesson on the facts of life and she said about not experimenting with boys and how awful it was to have an illegitimate baby because nobody liked you then and you had to have the baby adopted and give it up and I thought then, that's what's happened to you. I ran out of the Domestic Science room."

"Oh, dear." Libby sighed and looked straight ahead of her. "Yes. You're right," she said after a long pause.

"Am I?"

"I had a baby. That's all."

"All? It's awful."

"Oh, dear. I didn't want you to know. Not yet. Mattie, it happens. To silly girls like me. I had to keep it from you, Mum said. I'm not respectable."

"Are you allowed in here, since you're not respectable?"

"Don't be silly."

"I'm not silly. Fidelma's having a baby. She got married to cover it up, I think. I heard Mum and Aunt Delia talking. Why couldn't you get married?"

Libby looked upset. Mattie wanted to comfort her but didn't know how. "Oh dear! This is so difficult. The father – he wasn't in a position to marry."

"I would have wanted to help you."

"Look, Mum won't let me talk about it. She doesn't want you to know. She didn't want me anywhere near you."

"Why not?"

"In case you do the same."

"How stupid. And it was her grandchild." Mattie knew how angry she sounded.

"Ssh! Keep your voice down. There's more to it than that."

"What d'you mean?" Mattie hissed.

There was something going on at the high altar which was not visible from where they were sitting. The organ music had stopped. There were more people in

109

the Cathedral now. Without warning, a choir began singing. It was Gregorian chant, like she had learned to sing at St Angela's. "Credo in unum Deum…"

"*I believe in God*'. Do you believe in God, Libby? God let you get a baby. I don't believe in him. Not after today. Or yesterday. It's all so cruel. Was there something wrong with the baby?"

"Not wrong. Different. She's half-caste."

"What's that?"

"Not totally the same colour as me. He was black, the father."

Mattie stared, and started to cry again. "A piccaninny! A piccaninny. You gave away a darling piccaninny. Like the black babies in Africa, I used to buy pictures of, for a penny, to save them. I used to buy black babies and you've given one away. You must be so sad."

"Ssh! Mattie, it's not like that. I didn't put her up for adoption."

The stifled wails stopped.

"She's with me."

Mattie took a deep breath as she took in this information. A smile began to creep over her face. She could feel it cracking through her misery. "With you? Living with you? A little girl?"

Libby nodded, her serious expression melting as a smile began in response to Mattie's change of mood.

"Can I see her? When was she born?"

"Not today. But I will arrange it. She was born the day you started at the Grammar School. At this precise moment, Mattie, I'm worried about you. Shouldn't you be at school? And does Mum know about this escapade? When I got your note, this morning, I thought there was something wrong with her. I thought she was ill or something."

Mattie apologised, but was not concerned about Mum. "Why can't I see her?"

"Because you must go back home. If you go now, you can get a train at a quarter-past eleven and get into school for afternoon lessons."

"I don't want to ..."

"If you want to see your niece, you must go home now. I'd rather Mum didn't know about any of this, if at all possible. She'd be furious."

"Libby?"

"No."

"I want to hear the music. It's like my old school. There were no worries there."

"If you go back to Victoria station, I'll tell you her name and arrange for you to meet her during your Whitsun holidays."

Mattie gave in. She leaned out of the window of the train at Victoria.

"Her name is Rosie," Libby told her, smiling up at her from the platform. "I'll see you at Whitsun, at the usual time."

To her disgust, by midday, Mattie found herself back at Sittendon station facing a long walk across the town to the Grammar School and the prospect of presenting herself there with no real excuse for her absence that she could use. She forced herself through the school gates. The first person she saw, running towards her across the playing fields, would have been the last person she'd have chosen at that moment, Lola Johnson.

"Watch'er, Mattie. Where you bin? Have you heard? About Barbara?"

"No. What?"

"She's adopted. Came up after you left yesterday. She was real upset, about giving away babies. Snooty cow." And Lola, ever on the muscle, bounced away. Rosemary appeared.

"What's this about Barbara?"

Rosemary linked her arm with Mattie's. "Where've you been? Where did you go yesterday?"

"Tell me about Barbara."

"Her Mum's been up the school. Barbara knew she was adopted but Miss Graham said babies were given away for adoption and Barbara didn't like the idea of being given away. Her mother says it was indelicate. Barbara looked terrible this morning. So do you, now I'm looking at you."

"Yeah. I'm not well, a bit."

"We wondered where you'd gone yesterday, after the facts of life. Good, wasn't it, what Lola said. But Barbara sort of took over, yelling and crying. No one asked about you. Lola did. She can be shocking, though, can't she? Miss Graham was looking for you. And Mr Shepherd wanted to know where you were this morning when he called the register."

Mattie smiled. It was good to know that she was not the only one to have felt that Miss Graham's awful warnings about illegitimate babies were clumsy. Yes, indelicate was the right word. Gosh, it was good to be back, even after only one morning. This was her world, overwhelming though it could be, and despite the worries, like algebra, that arose from it.

She went in search of Miss Graham first, in the Domestic Science Room. She explained she had a sister, "who had done that."

"Done what, Martha?"

"Had a baby without being married and my Mum didn't like it." Shame Mum, she thought, but not Libby.

"I am so sorry to hear that, Martha. I am sorry you were upset, too."

Mattie nodded. "Will you explain to Mr Shepherd for me? I needed a lie-in this morning."

CHAPTER EIGHT

That afternoon, Mattie left the school happy that both her morning's absence and the previous afternoon's rapid exit had been explained so easily. All the attention had been focused on Barbara whose mother had come to the Grammar School to complain about Miss Graham. In Mattie's view, it appeared that Barbara counted, as did Barbara's mother. Martha Dobson, who lived in a council house, did not count. There were good aspects to that

As she walked towards home, down the lane that led to Oakfield Road, Lola caught up with her.

"Why did you run out yesterday? Where you bin this morning?" Lola panted as she reached her. "Were you shocked by the facts of life or something?"

"No," Mattie sighed, not wanting that image of her. "Nothing like that. I just remembered something, that's all." She regarded Lola. How trustworthy was this girl? Lola would be the ideal person to ask to receive letters from Libby. She broke rules, did things she was supposed not to do. But could she keep a secret? Rosemary was too well-behaved to be asked that favour. Her mother would not approve and would most certainly find out. Lola was different.

"I might tell you. One day," Mattie said.

"Oh, go on."

"No, not now."

Lola's attention was conveniently diverted by Barry

Wood, from next door, making his brisk way up the lane. He said, "Hello," to Mattie and smiled at her.

Mattie responded and saw Lola's eyes light up as she eyed Barry's departing back. "Who was that?"

"Barry Wood. He lives next door to me."

"Does he? Did you see how pink he went? He's quite good-looking, isn't he?" Lola glanced back to Barry who had nearly reached the top of the hill.

"I suppose so," Mattie said.

"Can you get me an introduction?"

"Aren't we too young for that sort of thing?"

"I'll be fourteen in the Autumn. My older sister, Sofia, she left school at fourteen. Isn't it a shame we have to stay on past fifteen to sixteen?"

"That's because we've got to take our O-levels."

"Yeah. O-levels. It'll be all O-levels all the time from September. They change our forms, you know."

"Yes. I think so." Mattie paused on the corner of the road. "I've got 'Girls' Crystal' indoors if you would like it."

"M'mm. I don't know. I'm reading 'Woman's Own' now. I don't want to be a kid forever."

Mattie assumed she must have looked crestfallen, for Lola stopped and turned. "Would you like to come round to mine in the summer hols?"

"That'd be nice. When there's no homework." There would be the chance to assess whether or not to trust Lola with her secret.

Mattie let herself into the house. Mum was in the kitchen-diner, making tea. She glanced up to greet Mattie. Mum knew nothing about what Mattie had been up to, she was oblivious. No one had come down from the Grammar School to ask why Martha Dobson was

115

not at school this morning. Mattie watched her mother. To her surprise, she became aware of a feeling of pity for her. Mum was not well, had four children, one of whom had left home and her second was deceiving her in unsuspected ways. She must be so scared, Mum, that Mattie would grow away from her, and possibly, Frank too, with his ambitions to get into the Grammar School.

"Are you all right, Mum?"

"Yes, I am. It's been a nice day," and Mum actually smiled at her. Oh dear. Guilt. These days Mum never asked her or Frank if they went to confession. Mattie hoped she never would, ever again. All these secrets...

Frank attended his interview at the Grammar School. He had new long trousers, for the occasion, to hide his scabby knees. Mattie had never seen him so spruced up as she did on the morning of his interview. His hair was smooth, newly trimmed and his face shone. Mum fussed over him proudly.

* * *

Deception was becoming so easy. On the Thursday of Whit week, Mattie set off for the station to catch the train to London with her usual line, "A day out with my friends". She had written a note to Libby to let her know she had not forgotten, was excited to be meeting Rosie. The train was not so crowded this time as it would have been earlier in the morning. She was meeting Libby as usual, at twelve o'clock. At Victoria, she leapt off the train and all but ran up the platform and yes! there was Libby at the ticket barrier, carrying Rosie. Mattie had a shock. She was expecting to see a baby in Libby's arms. But Rosie had been born on the day Mattie had started the Grammar School so she was nearly two years old now.

Libby, leaning to enable her to balance Rosie on her hip, was more than smiling, she was laughing. Mattie hurried up to her, embraced her sister and the not-so-little Rosie in one big hug. Rosie let out a protesting wail.

"She's lovely," Mattie said, her eyes feasting on the bonnie girl with a turned down mouth and reproachful big, brown eyes. "Doesn't she like me?"

Libby laughed. "She doesn't know you, Mattie. Rosie, this is your Auntie Mattie."

Rosie turned not only her face but her whole little body away from Mattie.

"I want her to like me."

"Of course you do. She will, once she gets to know you. Shall we go to the cafe?"

"With Rosie?"

"I can hardly park her like she's a bike! Mattie, I need to explain a few things." They walked to the cafe where they usually had a snack lunch. This time Libby ordered tea for both of them. She sat in a way that prevented Rosie's eager little hands from exploring everything on the table. This was irritating as Libby's attention was divided.

"I want to tell you about where I live," Libby said.

"In Greenwich?"

"In Greenwich. Did you ever hear of Auntie Grace?"

"Auntie Grace? No. Who was she?"

"She's Dad's sister."

"Dad's sister? I didn't know Dad had a sister."

"He has. He doesn't see her because Mum disapproves of her."

117

"Mum disapproves of lots of people."

"This is for a reason. Auntie Grace, she went to prison."

"Prison? Gosh! Why? Oh, Mum wouldn't like that."

"For procuring an abortion."

"What's that mean? Oh, I think I know."

"It's stopping a woman having a baby once it's started to grow."

"Inside her? So's the girl doesn't have it?"

"That's it."

Rosie was not happy with her mother giving a lot of attention to her aunt. Libby tried to distract her by handing her a teaspoon, which she promptly threw to the floor. Libby lifted her and turned her to face the opposite direction.

"How do they do that?"

"You don't need to know that. It's illegal."

"So how did anyone find out?"

"The girl died. It's the reason it's illegal. It's dangerous."

Mattie stared in shock. "That's awful. Gosh, that's really awful. So she went to prison. Miss Graham didn't say anything about that."

"Miss Graham?"

"My teacher. Domestic science. And the facts of life."

"Of course not. But there's more to tell you."

Mattie had noticed something that made her feel uneasy. A man and a woman, sitting at a nearby table, were watching Libby with Rosie, their eyes hard, mouths grim, as though Libby had done something wrong. "Libby," she whispered, "why's that couple glaring at you?"

Libby turned, then turned back again quickly. "Oh!" she muttered. "Mattie, pay the bill, will you?" She rose and slapped some coins onto the table. Clutching Rosie, she all but ran from the cafe. The owner of the cafe appeared at Mattie's side. She pushed the coins towards him and followed Libby.

"What happened?"

Libby was standing some yards from the cafe, out of sight of it. Her face was buried in Rosie's curly black hair. She was clearly upset.

"People disapprove. Of Rosie."

"Because she's coloured?"

"She's not coloured. She just a bit different from most people here. She is mixed. You're coloured. Pink." Libby's voice was fierce. "Come on. Let's get to Greenwich. As we wait for the bus, I'll tell you more."

"More?" Mattie rushed to keep up with her. "You're taking me to Greenwich?"

"Yes. Auntie Grace came out of prison. Mum wouldn't have anything to do with her and has made it impossible for Dad to see her. But – and here's the bit that's really tough – when I told her I was expecting my Rosie, she was only too keen for me to go to see Auntie Grace."

"Mum was? Libby, that's awful. To do an abortion? You might have died."

"I wasn't going to risk that. Mum had already been in touch with her. Auntie Grace wrote to me to tell me what Mum had said. She also said she would do no such thing. She offered me a home instead."

"Auntie Grace? In Greenwich? Is that where you live?"

"Me and Rosie." Libby was smiling. "It's quite

119

something for me to be telling you all this. I hope it's not too much for you."

"No, no. But Mum…"

They had reached the bus stop. Libby hailed a trolley-bus. Mattie had never been on a trolley-bus. The ride was smooth and quiet. Two poles from the roof were attached to overhead wires, carrying electricity. The conductor was from Jamaica, Libby said afterwards. He was very dark with large white teeth. Mattie smiled at him. She didn't want him to think she was like the couple in the cafe. Sadness rushed over her. Libby's life was so full of trouble. Poor Libby, poor Auntie Grace. And poor Mattie, with yet more secrets.

"Yes, Mum," Libby agreed. "She would help, but not in the way I wanted. Auntie Grace has been wonderful. She's an invalid. She lives on the ground floor. And I look after her. The upstairs is mine. It's not always the people who try to be virtuous who act virtuously, is it?"

"I'm finding life quite confusing at times. Like the way Mum treats you. That's not right, is it?"

"I've needed to explain about you to Auntie Grace. She was a bit worried at first. She thought you might tell Mum and then there'd be all hell to pay. But she's okay."

"I see what you meant when you said a lot of people could be hurt. But it's not by you, Libby, is it? It's Mum."

Libby shook her head. "I don't know why she's like it, why she is so unforgiving."

Auntie Grace turned out to be a very ordinary Londoner. She hobbled around on two sticks. Mattie was made welcome by her. She asked no questions about the family, not even Dad. Mattie searched to see the likeness but failed to do so.

120

After meeting Auntie Grace, she was taken upstairs to the rooms Libby and Rosie occupied. The sitting room had been furnished to Auntie Grace's taste, in styles fashionable long before the war. Everything was brown or sludge green. The bay window looked over a street of Edwardian terraced houses, with gaps of rubble and weeds where bombs had fallen.

A light meal of vegetable soup followed by apples and custard was prepared by Libby. Rosie was put down to sleep in the sitting-room downstairs and Auntie Grace watched over her while Libby took Mattie back to Victoria on the trolley-bus.

"Mum should see Rosie," Mattie said.

"I know. I wish she could. I think she doesn't know she exists and if she did she would so disapprove, like the couple in the cafe. So, unless it's impossible, please, not a word to Mum."

"She's got two lots of shame, hasn't she, you having Rosie and then suggesting you got rid of her. She's a darling, little Rosie. Oh, and Mum would disapprove because of Rosie not being pink."

After having given her more money for her fare for the summer visit, Libby waved good-bye from the ticket barrier.

* * *

One day in June, in the middle of the exams, Mattie reached home to find huge excitement in the house. A letter had arrived announcing that Frank has gained a place at the Grammar School. She could not help resenting that there was not this amount of jubilation when the same letter had come for her two years ago.

Frank's letter was displayed on the kitchen table, along with its enclosures, even the grant application form, for all to see. Mattie began to read it, then gave up in exasperation.

"You didn't make all this fuss when it was me," she said.

"It's more important for a boy," Mum said.

"Why?" Mattie said.

"Stop asking stupid questions. When he grows up, he'll have a family to support, not just himself, for a while, like you. You'll be supported by your husband."

"Suppose I don't get one?"

"Are you daft? Don't you want to get married?"

Mattie wanted to say that she didn't if this sexual intercourse was as rude as it sounded but refrained. Perhaps for Mum it was like that, and for Libby it wasn't.

By the time Dad eventually arrived home that evening, Frank was desperate to claim his attention and approval. Dad took everything in his stride, even his children gaining places at the Grammar School. Mattie was comforted to see his response to Frank's news was cool and detached, as it had been to hers two years previously.

"So we've got two little commies coming along," he teased.

"George!" Mum said.

"Well, it's well known. That fellow, Shepherd, he's a communist."

Mattie looked up from her half-hearted homework. "Not Mr Shepherd? You don't mean Mr Shepherd?"

"Shepherd. That's the fellow."

"No, you can't mean Mr Shepherd. He so nice."

Dad laughed. "Of course he is. You don't influence people by being unpleasant."

"Oh, George! This is Frank's turn, not Mattie's. Don't spoil it for him."

"It's not spoiled," Frank said. "Commies, swots, creeps, snobs, I'll deal with them all."

Mattie gave Frank a serious look. "You've got no idea, have you?" she said, shaking her head. This news about Mr Shepherd was unsettling. Yet, she was not to be under Mr Shepherd's influence for much longer. The day the exam week ended, a letter was brought home from school about Mattie's future. Mr Shepherd had explained it to 2B at one of the special meetings the form had with him. Mattie relayed it all to her parents.

"I'm changing form in September," she began, then realised all that meant to Mum was something to do with racing.

"My class," she added.

"You're going up?" Mum said.

Mattie drew a patient breath. "We're all going up. We'll all be Third Years in September. But we are being re-organised. Instead of being forms 2, 2A and 2B, we're going to be 3L, that's for languages, 3S, for sciences, and 3G, for general. That means domestic science, and woodwork for boys."

Mum looked up anxiously from the letter. "It says here we have to choose."

"Yes. I want languages. It's for O-levels, you see. It's the subject we are going to take at O-level. In three years time we will take our O-levels."

"What are they?"

"Exams."

"Oh, I see. But it says here we can let the teachers

123

choose. Surely they know what you're best at?"

"I want languages. You learn French, German and Latin if you go into the languages form."

"This is about what you're going to do when you leave school, isn't it?" Dad said and Mattie knew an opinion was coming up.

"Sort of." Mr Shepherd had talked about education at the form meeting. It was not, he said, all about jobs. It was about life. Mattie was confused. Perhaps she should forget about Mr Shepherd. Dad had spoken about dangerous ideas.

"I see," Dad said. "You won't need Latin, will you? Bob Grainger's daughter went to the Grammar School. She works in a bank now. And she's getting married soon. I think you should do domestic science."

"I want languages!"

"Now don't start," Mum said.

Too late. She had already started. Mattie wanted languages.

"Tell you what," Dad said. "I think we should let the teachers choose. They know what you're best at."

Everyone knew she was good at French so Mattie gave in for the sake of peace and agreed to that. The option, for parents to allow the school to choose, was marked, the letter went back to school.

The exam results and the Third Year form re-organisation were announced at another form meeting by the soon-to-be-parted-from Mr Shepherd.

This year, Mattie had done less well in the exams and there was a slight shift in her positions in the year's work too. Even in French, her best result, she came seventh.

"I don't know what happened to you, Martha."

Mattie gazed the desktop. "I do," she muttered. Libby, she thought. And Rosie.

It was the same with other subjects, except oddly, Maths. "Fifteenth, Martha Dobson. Well, that's a lovely surprise, Martha, all the extra work has paid off."

Mattie was furious. This was not how she wanted to see herself. The whole year's results showed the same slip in most subjects but not quite so marked. In French she was third. In maths, again there was an improvement. She was Fourteenth. Mr Watts' extra tuition had certainly paid off.

Then came the announcement about the new Third Forms. She listened intently for her name as Mr Shepherd read the 3L list first. Rosemary was there, so was Drusilla. Mattie, Barbara and Lola Johnson were not. When he read out the list for 3S, Mattie's name was first on the list, then came Conor Flynn and Lola Johnson. Barbara had been relegated to Domestic Science, or 3G. She was upset.

Mattie was furious again. She cried during break. "I don't want to do beastly science, I want to do languages, with you," she told Rosemary.

Rosemary tried to comfort her. "If you tell your parents, they'll ask for it to be changed. My Mum would."

Mattie had a feeling that in her case, her parents were different. "Anyway, 3S is full of boys. There are far fewer girls. I don't want to go there."

"Boys. Lola Johnson will love that," Rosemary tried and failed with a little humour.

Mattie tried and failed with her parents. The whole evening was devoted to the issue. Even the washing-up after tea was forgotten.

125

"They know what they're doing," Mum said, "we haven't a clue about any of it. They know all about these levels. They don't want people like us interfering."

"I told you what I wanted," Mattie said. "I told you."

"What you want and what is best for you are often two different things."

"Not in this case." Mattie raised her voice for emphasis.

Mum was appalled. "Really, Mattie, you are becoming very difficult."

"No, I'm not. It's because you don't listen to me."

"You don't know everything."

"I know more than you..." Mattie rose to her feet.

"Now, don't start that one." Mum stood up too, as if to say that the discussion was over.

"I'm not. All I was saying is, I know more than you what I want, what I enjoy. Why don't you ever listen to me? Why? Why?" She stamped her foot and brought her fist down on the table.

"There's no need," Mum began.

"Yes, there is! Yes, there is! You didn't listen to Libby either and look at the damage you did there!"

The silence was electric.

"You take that back, my girl," Mum said, all cold and steely. Then she raised her hand when Mattie did straight-line mouth back at her with hard glaring eyes. The next thing Mattie knew was a stinging slap on the side of her face that made her ears buzz and sent her reeling across the room.

"There's no need for that, Rita," Dad said, all calm.

"What she needs is some discipline," Mum muttered.

"Discipline is not the same as punishment, is not the same as torture," Mattie yelled.

"The girl's getting out of control," Mum said. "She'll end up in Borstal."

Mattie grabbed her school satchel and bolted out of the back door.

* * *

She stayed out as late as she dared. The evening air cooled her slapped cheek and made goose pimples rise on her arms. She wished she had the courage to go into the woods and stay there so she could hear the owls hooting. But Mum and Dad would call the police. There had been talk of that on the day she had run out of school about Libby. She knew she would have to go back home. She wandered around the estate, looking at the new houses going up on fields, where larks used to rise and sing on the wing. The memory upset her and made her want to cry.

On the way back she passed Lola Johnson's house. The lights were on, the windows open. Voices wafted on the still air. The house was alive with noise, movement, life and light.

Mattie returned home, creeping in through the back door. No one came to meet her. Up the now carpeted stairs (HP – they must owe hundreds, her Mum and Dad), to her room. She visited the bathroom, still a joy, then undressed and slipped into bed. They weren't worried about her, not one bit. She couldn't sleep.

* * *

Term had ended. There had been a Parent's Evening that Mum and Dad had been 'unable' to attend. Mattie begged them to go to ask for her form to be changed. "Ask them for me, Mum," she pleaded. "Ask them to put me in 3L, please."

"If it's that important to you, ask them yourself. You're there every day."

But Mattie thought that to question the teachers' decisions would have been the most appalling nerve.

Mr Shepherd had been said 'good-bye' to, with mixed feelings for Mattie. She understood she was to have him for Biology in 3S. The tension at home dissipated, although she was on tenterhooks about the school uniform now. As well as Frank's needs, there was a new skirt to be obtained for her. Gym slips were discarded as the serious study was beginning and skirts with stockings, (plus suspender belts) were the requirement.

With the end of term came the end of what Mattie thought of as romantic misty mornings that encouraged her to get up. They were replaced by scorching summer blue skies or the still and heavy atmospheric threat of thunderstorms.

Dad came up on the football pools. He indulged in this minor gambling every week. The family suffered in silent tension when the results were read out on the wireless on Saturday evenings. It was not that anyone had any hope of winning a fortune. The agony was waiting for Dad to snarl, "bloody Fulham," or "bloody Arsenal," the latter sounding heavily rude, the way he said it. Nobody was allowed to speak. The amount of the win was small compared to his dreams but enough to pay off some of the hire purchase debt and for a few treats. He took the family for a day out to Ramsgate, the scene of his childhood escape from hot days in London school holidays

They went by train. The boys were excited. Trips on trains were rare for them. They admired the engines at the station. Mattie laughed when they complained about smoke and smuts in their eyes as they tried to defy Mum and lean out of the window.

"Trains might be exciting," Mattie couldn't help saying, "but they are dirty." She watched the dizzying up-and-down of the telegraph wires beside the railway lines thinking of her trips to London to see Libby and Rosie. Before they reached Ramsgate, a man in American air force uniform boarded the train.

"He's coloured," Mum whispered to Dad. "What's he doing here?"

"He's American," Dad whispered back. "From Manston. USAF base here."

"I thought Americans were white." Mum was still whispering.

Rage rose up in Mattie's throat as she thought of Mum's granddaughter.

"Pink!" she rasped at Mum, who looked at her in puzzlement.

Since Dad's childhood visits to Ramsgate, the town had been ravaged by war and the after effects of it. He was upset to see the bomb sites in terraces of Georgian houses.

"It's like the place has had its teeth knocked out," he said. "And the modern replacements, well, they're just rubbish compared."

Mum made a beeline for the Abbey and its church, perched on the cliff top, with France across the sea. Mattie stood gazing at the smudge on the horizon. It was foreign and held the prospect of something new and challenging. In the Fourth Year, she would have a chance to go to France on a school exchange visit. Mum was uneasy at the number of black American airmen in Ramsgate. Mattie regarded her with contempt. She had to fight hard to resist the urge to the accuse her of 'colour prejudice'.

The summer holidays, in the new house, were memorable that year. Mum was in better health, Mattie had tea at Rosemary's and Rosemary came to tea at Oakfield Road several times. Mattie visited Lola, along the road. Lola talked fashions, film stars, television and women's magazines. She watched the Johnson's television on occasions. There was singing and dancing and lots of sparkle and glamour.

They came to an agreement, she and Lola. It was Mattie's idea.

"When term starts," she said, "will you help me with my maths, especially algebra. If you do, I'll help you with English."

Lola looked up from her preoccupation with 'Women's Own', with gratitude. "Oh, if you could. Can't make head or tail of this parsing stuff."

"You mean 'adverbial clauses of time', and things."

"Yeah. Rubbish."

For Mattie, there was a visit to Greenwich at the end of July. The visit lasted only long enough for a quick meal, but to Mattie, these visits were the one event in her life she anticipated with real eagerness. It was for the July visit that she first 'borrowed' some small change from Mum in order to buy a present for Rosie, sneaking it out of her purse when she was out of the room.

"Are you getting pocket money, now?" Libby asked with a frown on receiving the gift of a small teddy bear for Rosie.

"Dad had a win on the pools," Mattie said and was thankful that Libby asked no further questions.

Later in the school holiday, Mattie saw, on the Johnsons' television set, reports of the flood disaster at Lynton and Lynmouth in Devon.

"It was dreadful," she told Mum. "All this water, rushing down, washing people away in their homes. I remember when we were at Ramsgate, the water, as we paddled, tugging round my ankles. It was so strong."

"Don't upset yourself," Mum said, disturbed by this emotional response. "These things happen."

"They said it was an Act of God. I don't believe God would do that. If he does, I'm not going to believe in him."

THIRD YEAR
1952-53

CHAPTER NINE

Because of Dad's win on the pools, there was no agony over the skirt, stockings and suspender-belt for the new term, the start of the Third Year. Frank did not experience the worry about his school uniform that Mattie had had. The grant was easily dealt with. Mum did not feel the same shame when she filled in the form.

Whether it was being in the Third Year, or still result of a sort of waking up of feelings on seeing the film *'Limelight'*, Mattie did not know. Her awareness of world events led to an intense questioning of Dad on the Sunday lunch after the first British test of nuclear weapons in early October.

"The world I'm being educated for is not all lovely and beautiful as grown-ups pretend," she said on learning about Hiroshima and Nagasaki.

"You don't have to grow up waiting for nuclear war," Dad said.

"Yes, I do," she said. "I'm wondering if all is preparing for O-levels for three years is worth it, if we're going to be blown to smithereens by the Russians."

"Don't talk nonsense," Mum said.

Frank, who had just discovered algebra, or rather, algebra had been imposed on him, looked up. "Is there going to be another war?" His usually mischievous face had an anxious expression. "Just as I start the Grammar School."

Everyone laughed, for a few seconds.

The birth of Fidelma's baby, in October, caused some excitement in the family. Mattie observed sadly the jubilation over the birth on the first acknowledged child of the next generation in the family. What a pity Grandma had not lived long enough to see her first great-grandchild, Delia said. What a pity, Mattie wanted to say, that no one knew about Rosie. On Libby's behalf, she did her best to ignore baby Gerard Ignatius Kevin Parrott.

The next event to consume Mattie's newly awakened attention to the news was the Harrow rail crash. So light-heartedly had they made the day-trip to Ramsgate by train. The father of her maths teacher, Mr Watts', had been on one of the trains. He told the form, in fact, he told every form he took, so shocked was he, "My father went around in a daze and two hours later he came to and found all his pockets full of broken glass."

Mattie felt for Mr Watts. Her sympathy consumed her. She paid little attention to lessons that day. Dreadful things happened to people. Life was awful.

* * *

The arrangement between Mattie and Lola supporting each other with algebra and English, started well. Mattie's visit to Lola's house was interesting, especially the way Lola explained algebra, which was in a way Mattie could understand. She hoped it would make sense to Mr Watts. The Johnsons' house was chaotic. The television was switched on most of the time, there was noise and interruption from Lola's brother and sister, to-ing and fro-ing through the living room and talking all the time. Yet still the homework was done.

But it was the return visit to Mattie's home that was not so successful. Mattie and Lola sat side-by-side on Mattie's bed in the small bedroom. After she left, Mum came up to Mattie's room, her mouth in that dreaded straight line.

"I don't like that girl," Mum said.

Mattie looked up in surprise. "Lola? She's okay. Why don't you like her?"

"She's common," Mum said.

"Common? You say that about people you don't like. What does it mean?"

Mum shrugged. "I don't know. Coarse. Not very well bred, I suppose."

"Are we common?"

"Of course not."

Mattie burst out laughing. "There are a lot of girls at school who would think me common."

"Don't be silly."

"I'm not being silly. The girls who live on Gracehill, for instance. They'd say I was common, if I asked them."

"Is that because you're friends with that Lola?"

"No. I wasn't friends with Lola until after the move here."

"Oh, you just want an argument," Mum said and flounced out of the room.

Mattie jumped up to follow her. "I'm not arguing, Mum. I want to discuss this. I don't know what you mean by common."

"You want to be clever. You think, just because you go to the Grammar School, you can…"

"'Just because you go to the Grammar School,'" Mattie recited.

"You think you're clever!" Mum flared.

"I thought that was the idea of going."

"Not if it means having no respect for your parents."

* * *

As Christmas drew closer, some PT lessons were used for teaching ballroom dancing, much to Lola's delight. The conversation, for the girls, in all the three Third Year forms focused on party dresses.

"I have some extra money put aside for a Christmas party dress," Dad said, "from the pools' win."

"Oh, Dad!" Mattie was overwhelmed. "Thank you. You are so kind."

"I can afford to be kind this year," he said. "So no panics."

"I'll come with you to buy it," Mum said.

Which was what happened, one Saturday towards the end of November, not long before the Christmas visit to Libby. Mum took Mattie into a dress shop, one, she told her she'd had dreams of going into for herself.

"I want one of the new style dresses with a circular skirt," Mattie said.

"We shall see."

Mum spoke to the assistant. "My daughter needs a nice dress for a Christmas party."

The assistant searched the rail for inspiring examples, including a little tartan dress with puff sleeves and Peter Pan collar, which failed to inspire Mattie at all.

"Have you got a dress with a circular skirt?" Mattie said.

The assistant and Mum exchange looks. "We have.

I'm not sure they're what you want." She went to the back of the shop to return with the very thing Mattie had in mind. The skirt stood out and was a complete circle, she could see, when she held up a corner of the hem

Mum made a noise.

The assistant responded to the hint. She fingered the skirt. "Yes, they're lovely and stiff now but when you wash them, they're like paper."

Mattie gazed at it, with its pattern of green leaves and red flowers which would go with the red shoes from last year, and was just right for Christmas. She didn't want it for washing. She wanted it for the Christmas party.

"It's lovely. It will go with my red shoes."

Mum made a noise again.

"You have to remember your Mum's paying, dear," the assistant said.

"No, she's not. It's Dad who's paying. It's an early Christmas present. I want it."

There was no argument after that. They left the shop. Mum did not say a word. She was livid.

CHAPTER TEN

The celebration of the New Year was exactly the same as it had been last year. A precedent had been set then. Barry Wood appeared on the doorstep with his lump of coal, the Dobson family trooped round to the Woods' house, where they were offered Babycham. Last year it had been cider. Mattie tried some but was not impressed, though she didn't say so. Barry Wood tried to engage her in conversation which was mostly about boys' stuff. She noticed her mother's repeated glances in her direction. Once, her eyes met Mum's, whose mouth began to go into the straight line that was always a negative message. What was its Libby had said? "She's afraid of you doing the same thing."

Seeing Mum's expression, Mattie began to feel fury rising, or perhaps it was the Babycham. Her face grew hot. Then she thought she might have a little fun. She turned to Barry and asked a lot of questions about cars.

"Would you like to be a racing driver?" she found herself saying.

"Yes," he said with shining eyes. He was trying to be a man of few words.

"I often think what fun it would be to sit in an open topped car, my hair flying, speeding along the road." She flicked her hair with her fingers and laughed loudly, less at the prospect she had described, more at the sight of Mum's face.

"I've been invited to a party," she went on, "It's on

Twelfth Night. Along the road. Lola Johnson's house. D'you want to come?"

"That sounds nice," said the man of few words.

Mattie returned home, satisfied that she had fulfilled a longed for request of Lola's which would put her in a position of being able to ask for a favour for herself.

Mum said nothing as they walked back home. She had already made her feelings clear. Mattie went to bed, planning to wear the dress with the circular skirt, once more, on Twelfth Night. She had not even planned to accept Lola's invitation.

On Twelfth Night, Barry waited for her at the end of the front garden path. Lola's joy at seeing Barry on her doorstep was a reward in itself. The party was noisy, with records playing, lots of Babycham and smoking, cakes and biscuits, sugar having come off the ration recently. There were boys there, including Conor Flynn, but neither he nor Mattie were ready to indulge in the behaviour later to be observed in Lola and Barry. Mattie and Conor sat and talked about school. It was the only thing to do. She did not particularly like him and he did not seem to be interested in her, other than as a school friend. Lola, with Barry, was different. Mattie came across the two of them, sprawled on the floor of the landing upstairs, their bodies entwined, Lola's skirt pushed up well beyond her knees, kissing Barry, his hands in places that were shocking. She went home, long before the Babycham was exhausted and only little less than sober. Mum was waiting for her, sitting on the stairs in her dressing gown, even though she wasn't well.

"There you are," she said, dragging herself to her feet. Her eyes swept over Mattie's intact clothing, unruffled hair. "You behaved yourself, I hope."

"Mum, of course I did. Why do you always expect the worst?"

"Because I've seen it happen."

This was one of only a few references she had ever made to Libby.

* * *

In November, on Mattie's last visit to Libby, they had arranged for her to go again in January. Libby's birthday was in January. Mattie took an avid interest in the weather forecasts on the newly acquired television set, yet another of the blessings bestowed by the win on the football pools. That snow might prevent the journey was her biggest anxiety. Money Libby had given her had already been spent on some scented soap as a birthday present for her and she realised she would need to borrow some from Mum's purse. She watched for an opportunity, which came when Mum went out to the coal shed for more coal.

"What d'you think you're doing?"

The voice shocked Mattie. It was Mum. She stood there, in the sitting room doorway with the coal scuttle. Mattie, stooping over the handbag, her hands hovering above it, froze.

"Oh! I just – just I, tripped, I tripped over it. The handle. I nearly tripped." She straightened. "It's dangerous, leaving it there on the floor. You should put it somewhere safe."

Mum came right into the sitting-room. Mattie, hot and bothered, left it. She crept upstairs to her bedroom. There, she sat on the bed, weak and tremulous. She had to do something and there was only one thing left for her to do. Lola lived down the road. A short visit to her would solve the problem.

So after tea, that evening, she wrapped up against the cold night and called on Lola.

"I need to ask a favour," Mattie said, close to tears. "And I don't like asking it."

"Is it something illegal?"

They were in Lola's over-crowded, over-stimulating bedroom which was a riot of colours, decorations and sparkle, fairy lights and tinsel hanging everywhere. Except for the posters of film stars, torn from magazines, that filled every wall space, it was like Santa's Grotto.

"No, not illegal. But my Mum doesn't know about it."

"Will it take long? I'm seeing Barry at eight. I'm going to his house. To watch TV."

"No, it'll be very quick. I need to give someone your name and address for them to write to me without my Mum knowing."

Lola grinned. "A boy?"

About to say "no", Mattie thought again. Lola would understand illicit correspondence with a boy. There would be no need to explain to her about Libby. "Don't tell anyone," she said.

"Not likely," Lola said. "Fine. Put my name and address on any letters. Tell him to write it to 'Lola and friend', then I won't open it. I can give it to you at school. Is that who you were going to see when I met you on the train that time?"

That was a long time ago, Mattie thought. But she nodded, assenting to yet another lie.

At home she composed a short note to Libby.

Dear Libby,

I am sorry to ask. Can you send money for my fare on Saturday, please? I have run out. I got you a birthday present. Please send it to my friend. Address it to Lola Johnson and friend, 2, Oakfield Road. The rest is the same as ours. She thinks I've got a boy friend in London so your secret is still safe with me.

Love to you and Rosie from Mattie xxxx.

She put the note in an envelope that was left over from a Christmas card, used one of her supply of stamps kept for this predicted emergency and addressed the envelope to Libby. The next morning, on her way to school, she made a short detour to the nearest pillar box.

The reply came, through Lola, not the next day but the day after that. Two one pound notes had been slipped in an envelope with a short note.

Libby's birthday was on a Friday, so Mattie's visit was on the next day. This time, she was to make her own way to Greenwich. She knew where to wait for the trolley-bus, which one to catch and where to alight.

As she approached Auntie Grace's house, she could see, in the upstairs bay window, Libby, with Rosie, watching and waiting for her. She waved. By the time she had reached the house, the front door was open and they were there. Rosie stood holding Libby's hand, her eyes looking up at Mattie.

"Atty!" she said.

Mattie wanted to cry. "She remembers me. Does she? Does she really remember me?"

"I'm not sure." Libby greeted her with a hug and a kiss. "I've been telling her all morning that Mattie is

144

coming. I think she'll want to sit on your lap this time. Pop into the kitchen to say 'hello' to Auntie Grace, then come upstairs to my sitting-room."

Mattie went upstairs to the sitting room, negotiating the gate at the top of the stairs and the toys strewn on the floor there.

"Now, Mattie," Libby began, sounding a bit like Mum. "I've told you before, you don't have to buy me or Rosie presents. I know how difficult it is for you, coming here, not telling Mum and all that. Just to see you is the biggest gift you could ever think of."

"Sorry," Mattie mumbled, recalling the close shave when she'd tried to gain access to Mum's purse.

"So how is everyone?" Libby said.

"Frank has settled down at school," Mattie said, reaching out to lift Rosie onto her lap. "I'm coping quite well. Lola, the friend you sent the money to, she lives in our road. She breaks rules easily. She helps me with my algebra."

"Can she keep secrets?"

"She ought to. I introduced her to Barry next door and she's going out with him now. And she thinks when you write to me that you're a boy".

"And Mum?"

"She's okay. I think she's not been too well since Christmas."

"She's probably going through one of her phases when she doesn't feel so good. And Dad?"

"He's always the same, is Dad. You're twenty-one now, aren't you? You'll be able to vote. And you can get married without having to ask Mum and Dad's permission, can't you?"

"If I ever find someone to take on me and Rosie."

"Button," Rosie said, tugging the buttons on Mattie's cardigan.

"Ah, isn't she sweet? Who am I, Rosie? Who am I?"

"Atty!" Rosie wriggled in delight.

"I made a card for you," Mattie said as she pulled out sheets of folded paper from her handbag.

Libby unfolded them and read from them:

I dreamt I was in heaven
with mountains, owls and sheep,
And the two people I love the most
Libby and Rosie so sweet.

"That's lovely. Did you really dream that?"

"It's a daydream. Not a night-dream dream."

"Thank you. Do you write poems at school?"

"No! I wouldn't dare. For heavens' sake, I'm in the Third Year. It would be seen as soppy. There are more boys than girls in my form. We have music, to soften us up, the boys say. It's once a week and it's so interesting. I didn't know anything about classical music, but I'm really enjoying learning about it."

"So tell me about this Lola."

"She's in my form. She's a bit cheeky. Bold, you know. Mum doesn't like her. She says she's common. I'm not sure what that means any more. We had an argument about that, me and Mum."

"So who are your friends now as well as this Lola?"

"Rosemary, still. Lesser friends are Barbara and Drusilla. I don't see Carol now, only if I go round Woolworth's on a Saturday. She works there."

* * *

146

At school on Monday in response to Lola's casual query, "Did you have a good weekend?" Mattie was able to respond, "Yes, thanks to you."

"Any time," Lola said the conspiratorial grin.

At the end of January, there was a massive storm that travelled down the whole of the east coast and affected the south coast too. Lives were lost as the sea broke flood defences and towns were under several feet of water after fierce winds and torrential rain. Canvey Island, which Dad knew well, was in a distressing state. People died, were trapped on roofs, waiting to be rescued. Homes were lost. Mattie saw it all on the newly installed television. Dad was upset. Mattie wanted to cry. Why did such awful things happen to people?

Her short walk to school that morning was in heavy rain, under dark skies. In assembly, the hall lights were blazing, so dark was it. Everyone was damp, hair was plastered to foreheads, the floors were wet from sodden footwear, the atmosphere was heavy with warm moisture but no one could get warm.

The spring term, with no distractions, unlike Christmas and the Summer term, was a time of hard work. Mattie saw Rosemary out of school regularly and Lola often in the evenings for homework as well as for more frivolous conversations about film stars, and Radio Luxembourg.

At school it was an unmemorable year, the one in the middle of her school career, except for the Coronation, which the family was able to watch on television. Later the whole school was marched to the local cinema to see the occasion recorded in glorious Technicolor and that was repeated for the film of The Ascent of Everest.

Mattie's fourteenth birthday came and went. Visits to Libby and Rosie, who was gradually getting to know Mattie, were part of the routine in her life now.

* * *

"I don't understand it."

Mum was sitting at the table, on which were a teapot and cups and saucers. Her purse was before her, its contents, coins, spread out. She had a pencil in one hand that hovered over a used envelope, scrawled with crossed out calculations. Mattie had come in from school.

"What's wrong?" she said.

"I never have as much as I think I have. I'm two-and-six shorter than I was yesterday, and yesterday, I was two shilling shorter than I thought I was. But I haven't spent any money." She looked up at Mattie. "Do you know anything about this? Have you been helping yourself to my purse?"

Mattie went cold, then hot. She sat on the nearest chair. "No, Mum. I haven't. Honestly, I haven't."

Her heart was thumping. She recalled the occasion when Mum had almost caught her going into her handbag. She had not 'borrowed' any small change, not since then. Her protest was genuine.

"I only asked. After all, you go off with your school friends I never know where you go nor if you need money to spend. That time you went to the pictures, for example. Where did you get money for that?"

"I can't remember. When was that?"

"Near your birthday, last year."

"Yes, well. I had the ten shilling note that Libby left

148

on my dressing table the day she went."

"That's three years ago. You kept it all that time?"

"It was precious." Mentioning Libby's name was daring but it served as a diversion. Mum did the straight–line mouth. Mattie looked her in the eye. "Well, I miss her," she said. "Still."

Not wanting to deal with a response to that, she rushed upstairs to change out of her school uniform. She heard the boys come in, first Frank, then Tony. The sound of loud voices reached her, shouting even. When she went back downstairs to the kitchen-diner, she found Mum on her feet, wielding her big wooden spoon, Frank with his hand on the handle of the back door. Tony was leaning on the door frame to the hall, watching, the proceedings, with a smirk on his face.

"You should give us pocket money," Frank was shouting. "Everybody else has pocket money. It's not fair. I look stupid."

"What do you want pocket money for, at your age?" Mum raged.

From Tony came the answer, "Fags! They smoke in the bike sheds."

Tony fled up the hall as Mum turned to demand clarification. At the same time Frank darted out of the back door, up the rockery steps, and the garden path through the unconquered heaps of clay, to the top of the garden, where he vaulted over the chain-link fence.

Defeated, Mum sat down at the table again. She put her head in her hands. "I don't know what that Grammar School has done to you two," she said. "You're both unmanageable."

Mattie sat down beside her. "Mum, we're growing up. I'm fourteen. People used to leave school at

149

fourteen. Perhaps you shouldn't be managing us. Try loving us instead."

Mum looked at her, but avoided looking straight into her eyes. "I can't stand this superiority of yours." She took a deep breath. "You and Frank can stop having school dinners. I can feed you both more cheaply if you come home to dinner."

Mattie drew a breath to protest that not being in school at lunchtime would deprive her of time with her friends. Then she realised Mum would not see that as important. She decided to accept it and make the lunchtime visit home as short as possible.

* * *

She told her woes to Rosemary one lunchtime, having rushed back to school, eating a Spam sandwich on the way, much to Mum's disgust.

"I want to go on the French exchange visit," she said as they sat on the grass by the cricket field, "But I don't think my Mum and Dad can afford twelve pounds for me."

"I'm in a similar situation," Rosemary said. "It's a lot of money, twelve pounds."

"I've been thinking I could get a job. My friend Carol was getting five shillings for Saturday mornings in Woolworths. If I did a whole day, that would be ten shillings a week. By half term I'd have six pounds."

"I do my homework on Saturday," Rosemary said. "It would be a big upheaval."

"There's always more at the weekend, isn't there? I'm sort of busy some Saturdays," Mattie said. She did a rapid calculation. If she saw Libby and Rosie at half terms and school holidays, it might be possible to have a Saturday job.

"Let's go and look for a job on Saturday, in the shops in the town," Rosemary said and the bell sounded for the end of lunch break.

* * *

Mattie visited Libby and Rosie at half-term, in October.

"You don't look so happy this time," Libby said, scrutinising her face. "What's happening?"

Mattie, with Rosie on her lap, looked over the child's curly head. She sighed. "Nothing in particular. Everything in general. You know, in January, I passed the halfway mark in my time at the Grammar School. When I returned to school for the Autumn term in September, I was sixty percent through my time there. I'm in the Third Year, now. My form teacher, Mrs Andrews, told us it's a year of hard work and little excitement."

"You mean the excitement has worn off now."

"Long ago. And Mum's health has taken a slight turn for the worse. I find myself doing more and more chores."

"Don't the boys help?"

"You're joking! And I've realised that you're never coming back home."

"That wasn't ever on the cards."

"And Rosie's three and Mum's never seen her, doesn't even know that she exists. It's not right."

"Everything is all right at school, though, isn't it, apart from being a bit predictable and hard work?"

"There's one event on the horizon that I'm looking

151

forward to and that's the French exchange visit. We go there, and stay with the family of our pen-friends, who we don't know yet, and they come back to us. I don't think Mum likes it, either me going there in March or April, or the pen-friend coming here in the summer, though I've worked out how to solve the sleeping arrangements. Me and the pen-friend, we'd have the boys' room and they go into mine, with a camp bed for Tony."

"They won't like that."

"They'll have to put up with it." She pondered whether to mention the problem of money for the trip, but decided not to as it might seem like asking for it. She put Rosie down. She was beginning to feel upset.

"Why is life so difficult, Libby?"

"Is that how you feel?"

"Life seems to be more of a mystery than ever. I thought an education might give me some answers. Instead of that, I find more questions. There were so many demands on me, so many expectations. Not just at home, at school, too. My only consolation is music. I'm learning so much that's interesting about classical music, and hearing it too." She paused, sniffing back her tears. "Music is like somewhere, on which to put my feelings, how I feel about a confusing world. In music, I can hear that I am not the only person to feel so passionately about things, good things and sad things, and about life."

FOURTH YEAR
1953-54

CHAPTER ELEVEN

"I need to speak to Miss Dixon," Mattie told Rosemary. It was a chilly October morning.

"You just want to keep warm during break," Rosemary said. "It's better than going outside. Going to the staff room."

"That's one reason. The other is France. I'm so desperate to go. I do hate having to go to the staff room, though."

There were two staff rooms at the Grammar School, one for men teachers, in the western half of the building, and one for women teachers at the opposite end. The whole school was built around this separation. The girls' toilets and cloakrooms, the Domestic Science rooms as well as the women's staff rooms were at the eastern end. In Mattie's opinion the opposite end, where all the boys' facilities were, smelled different.

She knocked on the door of the women's staffroom and then had a humiliating wait before somebody opened the door. A face appeared in a narrow gap as though terrified of the pupils. Swirling cigarette smoke seeped out through the opening.

"Can I speak to Miss Dixon, please?"

"Miss Dixon," the anonymous face said and shut the door.

Mattie waited some more. Then the door was flung open, Miss Dixon, the French teacher emerged, carefully pulling the door nearly shut behind her, as though secrets might escape with the cigarette smoke.

"I'm sorry to bother you, Miss Dixon, but I want to talk to you about the French exchange."

Miss Dixon let the door close. She took a step forward. "Oh yes, Martha. Is there a problem?"

"Yes. The money. Twelve pounds is an awful lot of money. I don't think my parents can afford it."

"There are arrangements in cases like yours. The letter I sent home explains it."

Tears sprang to Mattie's eyes. "I didn't read the letter."

"I see," Miss Dixon said. "If they fill in the form you can go for eight pounds."

"That's still going to be difficult." Two big tears made their way down her face, one either side of her nose. She sniffed hard.

Miss Dixon moved to a darker corner. "Look, don't upset yourself. I'll think of something. The deposit is only two pounds. You have until the Spring half-term to pay the rest."

"You don't understand." Mattie was desperate now. "I live on Hill Common. We're all thick down there."

"Oh, Martha. That doesn't apply to you."

"That's the trouble," Mattie muttered, having found a handkerchief to not only to mop her tears but to hide behind too.

"Listen Martha, don't worry. I'll sort it out for you."

"They'll have to sign things, won't they, like for my passport and stuff."

"I'll come and see them."

"Oh, gosh, no," Mattie muttered into her handkerchief. "Thanks, Miss Dixon."

She dawdled her way back to Rosemary to give her

face time to recover from the tears. At lunch break, she went home in a hurry.

"Why didn't you tell me I can go to France for eight pounds?" she demanded as she burst through the door.

Mum was opening a tin of Spam. She shook it out of the tin onto a plate. "Because I can't find eight pounds any more than I can find ten pounds."

"Miss Dixon says I can go. She'll think of something. She'll come and see you."

"Oh, will she?"

"Yes. And if you're rude to her, I'll tell her about Libby."

Mum took the plate to the table. "You're fifteen next April. If I have any more of this attitude, I take you out of that school and you can get a job and earn your own money for your jaunts."

"It's not a jaunt," Mattie said quietly. Then she gave up. She eyed the Spam, the margarine and butter on the table. As soon as Mum's back was turned, she made herself a sandwich and left with it in her hand to eat as she made her way up the lane and back to school.

Two days later, Dad quietly gave her two one pound notes. "For France," he said. "I was there. In the war. The first one. You should see it."

"Thanks, Dad. Where did you get it?"

He tapped the side of his nose. She knew, somehow, telepathically perhaps, that he had borrowed it, maybe from Bob Granger.

"Mum's not well," he said.

She took the money to Miss Dixon. Now she had six pounds to find. In school that afternoon, Friday, the form 4S had its weekly music lesson. They were learning about Beethoven who had written a great deal of music so was being dwelt upon for several weeks. Today it was the Pastoral Symphony. Mr Smith, the music teacher, explained each movement then played the first, 'By the brook'. Mattie let the sounds carry her to a safe place, a beautiful place. The notes for the birds made her want to cry. She could see the woods and fields beyond the town, where the larks sang higher and higher, and the cuckoo called, always around her birthday. The scene wobbled through her teary eyes.

"Tomorrow," Rosemary said as they prepared to go home at the end of the day, "let's go and find a job for each of us. Shall I see you at the bus station, ten o'clock?"

* * *

They had both dressed to impress.

"Let's start with Woolworths," Rosemary said.

"I don't want to go to Woolworths. Let's go to Phillips'."

"The store we get our uniforms from? You're aiming high."

She was not so confident when she reached the store. She spoke to one of the suave men by the door. "I'm looking for," she hesitated while the right words settled into her brain, "employment," she finished grandly.

"They're not here," he told her. "Come back on Monday. Personnel is on the top floor. Near the hairdressers."

Mattie thanked him and reported back to Rosemary, who was researching the cosmetics counter.

"Come back Monday, he said. Can you come after school?"

They returned on Monday afternoon. To Mattie's delight they were both offered four hours on a Saturday for seven-and-six each, Mattie washing up in the cafe – not as smart as the restaurant – Rosemary in hardware, actually selling things, "like babies' enamelled chamber potties," she said.

The washing up was hard on Mattie's hands. She was provided with rubber gloves which helped. The other staff quite soon began sending her out to wipe tables and there were customers who were kind enough to give her a shilling tip for being thorough. Drusilla and her mother appeared one Saturday morning. Mattie had to go out to wipe clean their table before they sat down with much amusement, barely a thank you and certainly not a tip.

Head held high, her cheeks flaming, Mattie returned to her place, behind-the-scenes.

* * *

It had to be a French lesson, Mattie's absolute favourite. The school secretary tapped on the class room door. Miss Dixon went over to open it. She and the secretary had a brief whispered conversation before Miss Dixon called Mattie over.

Mattie went. Miss Dixon urged her through the door to the corridor before closing it. The secretary touched Mattie's upper arm.

"Martha, could you go home? A neighbour came up to the school to say your Mum's not well."

Mattie was angry. She pushed the door open into the classroom and stomped over to the desk to retrieve her satchel and her books.

159

"My Mum, not well," she muttered to Miss Dixon before charging out again.

When she reached home, Mrs Wood opened the front door.

"Is she bad?" Mattie said.

"Not good, love. She needs someone here. I should be at work, but luckily I heard her, banging on the wall. She's on her bed."

On, rather than *in* her bed. As Mrs Wood left, Mattie mounted the stairs slowly, so as not to give a message of panic. She pushed open the door of Mum's bedroom. The curtains were drawn, making it gloomy. The room smelt thickly, of sweat and warm body. There was Mum, eyes closed, on top of the eiderdown, in her day clothes. Her face was white. Mattie gazed at her for a few seconds. Mum looks small and vulnerable. How did such an insignificant-looking person wield so much power, and such fierce power too?

Mattie approached the bed. "Mum?"

The eyes opened with a reluctant flicker.

"Mattie? Oh, how nice of you." The voice was slow and low.

"What's wrong with you?"

"Oh, the usual. I just felt I couldn't go on, that's all. How did you get here?"

"Mrs Wood. She came up to the school. I had to leave my French lesson."

"I'm sorry." Mum shut her eyes again.

"Is there anything you need?"

"A cup of tea would be nice." Unpleasant reactions stirred in Mattie's resentful mind. Had she left her French lesson in order to come home and make her mother a cup of tea?

"I'll make your cup of tea. I don't know how ill you are, but it must be bad for you to send for me. So I think it's not a good idea to stay on top of the bed."

"No. I'm cold. There's no fire yet to warm the house. I haven't lit it."

"Why don't you take off your jumper skirt and get under the covers in your petticoat?"

Mum made no move.

"Do you want some help?"

"No, no. I'll manage."

Once downstairs, Mattie put the kettle on, measured tea leaves into the warm pot, filled the pot when the water had boiled then set about lighting the fire in the sitting-room. This new-fangled fireplace, as Dad called it, was supposed to warm the whole house, the flue going up the centre giving out heat in all four main rooms, but not Mattie's bedroom and the bathroom, both on outside walls.

She crouched down to riddle the grate, clean up the ashes, which had to be put in the ashcan to be spread on the path up the garden. Then, after taking a cup of tea up to Mum, who was propped up on pillows now, she went out to the coal shed to fetch coal and firewood. She came in, lit the fire, after she had found the matches. Sitting back on her heels, she watched as the fire roared behind its closed doors.

"You lit the fire," Mum said when she went back to her. "You are good." The praise was rare but Mattie's annoyance at the situation wouldn't let her accept it.

From the foot of the bed she said, "I'm not staying home all day, Mum. I'm going back to school this afternoon. It's music. I can't miss that."

"It's only this once."

"No. I need that music."

"How can you possibly need music? It's not useful."

"To me, it is. You don't know what hell my life is."

"You shouldn't be talking like that, at your age. It's only when you get older, like me, you can say that sort of thing. You don't know what hell my life is."

"I don't need to. Look, Mum, I'm not competing with you. I'm only trying to tell you something I'm convinced you don't know."

"Oh, I hate it when you talk like that, all superior."

Mattie moved towards the door. "It's half-past eleven," she said, glancing at the alarm clock. "I'll make you a sandwich and pour you another cup of tea. Then I'm off back to school."

When she arrived back at school, Lola, proving to be a really good friend, had notes for her on the French and Geography lessons she had missed. There were to be two more lessons that afternoon before music, the last lesson. Mr Smith, the music teacher, was still discussing and demonstrating the works of Beethoven. Form 4 S sat in an informal group as he darted from the blackboard, to the record player, to the piano. Mattie gazed out of the window. Conor Flynn, behind her somewhere, was whistling some of the themes that Mr Smith played on the piano before he put on the record of the first movement of the Ninth Symphony. She let the music wash over her, the passion in it, the enthusiasm, moving her to tears.

"Are you all right, Martha?" It was Mr Smith. The music had stopped. She looked up.

"Yes, I'm fine. I think I like Beethoven."

He smiled and it occurred to her that he must feel he was tolerated, he and his passion for music, rather than his efforts enjoyed or even appreciated, by most pupils.

162

Lola walked home with her. She chatted about the Christmas party, only weeks away now.

"People lie, don't they?" Mattie said.

Lola looked surprised at this change of subject. "Do they?"

"Yes. They tell you what's good and right, but they don't believe it. Work is supposed to be good. I still hate maths and my Saturday job is slavery. Growing up is supposed to be good, but I think it's hell. The Grammar School is supposed to be good, but sometimes I wish I could get out of it at fifteen."

"Then you'd have to go to work, which you say isn't really good."

"Suppose so. They want you to think that war is good, but I'm terrified of a war with atom bombs. They tell you to tell the truth but they lie themselves."

"Well, if you're right and we all agreed with it, we'd all give up, then where would we be?"

"Growing up is learning to be a liar."

"Hey, that's a bit much," Lola said, executing a twirl in the middle of the lane.

"Mothers are supposed to love their children."

"Yours does, doesn't she?"

"I suppose so. In her way. I just don't like her way, though."

"Is she cruel?"

"No. She doesn't mean to be. She's ill."

"Was she bad today? Was she very bad today?"

Mattie shrugged. "How would I know?"

"She's not very ill, though, is she, not at death's door? Or you wouldn't have come back, would you?" She stopped walking. "I go this way. Cheer up. It's the week end."

"I am cheered up," Mattie said thinking of Beethoven.

* * *

Christmas that year was spent at Delia's and by then Mum's health was much improved. Uncle Fred came in his car to fetch the Dobson family, Mattie, Mum and the boys were crowded into the back seat. Presents and contributions towards the festivities were put in the boot with much ceremony.

All over Christmas, Fidelma sat in a large armchair, cradling her baby, Gerard, and being fussed over. Mattie ignored them as much as possible, out of loyalty to Libby. Delia had taken up knitting, adopting Grandma's mantle, and promising to knit Mattie a cardigan for her school holiday.

"You won't be expected to wear school uniform will you, not on holiday?" Delia asked Mattie

Mattie tossed her head and tutted. "Of course not. It's not just a holiday, you know. It's not just for fun. It's to improve my French and to learn about France."

"I don't like the French," Delia said.

Mattie was about to protest at this, but stopped. It was Christmas, after all. She was there to celebrate the birth of Jesus by watching the uncles get blind drunk and the aunts very merry.

"Do you know any? French people I mean?"

"No. And I don't want to," Delia said.

"That's not very sensible," Mattie said.

"Oh, don't you start, with your Grammar School cleverness," Mum said.

Mattie raised her eyebrows. "What was clever about that?"

Mum did the straight-line mouth. Delia smiled unconvincingly. Fidelma smirked over her baby's head.

"Don't start, Mum," Mattie said quickly before Mum could reply. Exasperated, Mum turned away. Mattie smiled to herself. She had kept calm that time and she had not been squashed either.

CHAPTER TWELVE

By Christmas, Mattie had saved six pounds, from her wages, in National Savings stamps towards her French exchange holiday. In January she was able to pay the rest of the money for the French Exchange visit. Miss Dixon asked her how she had managed to find it.

"I have a job, Miss Dixon. In Phillips', in the cafe," she said. "I started by washing up but they promoted me to waitress since Christmas. I got a rise, too. I get eight shillings now."

"That's very good. I hope it's not detracting from your schoolwork, Martha?"

"It's alright. It's only Saturday mornings."

Rosemary had given up her job at Philips'. The bus journey from Milton Stanwick took too long. She then pulled out of the French Exchange visit because of lack of money.

"It's not money on its own. It's the sleeping arrangements," she said. "Where would the French girl sleep? There's no room at my house."

Mattie was disappointed. "I thought we'd enjoy it, going together. It's going to be a bit lonely for me." There was not enough room at her home either, Mattie knew, but she was not going to allow a small question like that to spoil her dream.

"Have you got the name of your pen friend yet?"

"Aline. Sounds boring, doesn't it? I was hoping for a Genevieve or a Violette."

After a long spell of severe weather, during which Mattie struggled to reach her job in the cafe, the day of departure for France was close. Mattie had earned a further four pounds since the New Year, some of which she spent on a present for Rosie and for necessities for the visit, not wanting to ask Mum. She changed the rest into francs. She sat on her bed, gazing at her passport, at the French francs, and the suitcase Mrs Wood next door had loaned her.

There had been no buying of new clothes for the trip, like Drusilla and Barbara. Delia gave her a skirt, along with the ghastly embroidered cardigan she had knitted especially for Mattie's holiday. The skirt had been Fidelma's, but was too small for her now as she had put on weight since having the baby. The new shoes Mum had obtained from the WVS. They were black with childish ankle straps which Mattie hid under the turnovers of her white ankle socks. Miss Dixon had advised taking some summer clothes as it was likely to be warm. They were going quite a long way south. A travel rug would also be needed for the overnight journey.

The coach picked up the party at seven o'clock in the morning, outside the Grammar School. Dad came with Mattie, to carry her case. She wore her school raincoat, which was now much shorter on her, over Fidelma's skirt, which was longer than the raincoat. She was not bothered by this until she saw the other girls in their best outfits, with nylon stockings and smart shoes. With that, and the absence of Rosemary, her optimism and sense of adventure evaporated. She was consumed by the feeling that she had failed to reach a standard she had not realised was expected.

She boarded the coach to be confronted by a sea of faces from whom she wanted to cringe. Without Rosemary, she was lost. Everyone else was sitting next to friends. The only person who was not, was Conor Flynn, not an exciting prospect. It was not as bad, though as the likelihood of choosing an empty seat and waiting to see if someone much worse than Conor would choose to sit beside her.

She opted for Conor.

"Is anyone sitting here?" she asked him.

"No," he said and turned his head to look out of the window.

They travelled in silence, she awkward, wishing she had not come. Halfway to Newhaven, she wondered if he was feeling the same way, even more so, perhaps, because a girl had chosen to sit next to him.

"I wish I hadn't come," Mattie said.

"Why?" he said, clearly not wanting to know.

"My friend Rosemary Hadlow, she changed her mind. All the others, they're kind of – you know." She knew he did know.

"Smarmy lot," he said and grinned.

She smiled, said nothing but sat back in her seat more relaxed. On the ferry, she explored alone, enjoying the experience of a slightly rough sea. The other girls, in their smart coats, threw themselves around, shrieking stupidly. On the train at Dieppe, she 'found' herself in the same carriage as Conor. He was better than being alone. He had forged his way ahead and was sitting by the window.

"Want a window seat?" he said as she came in. He moved along. She thanked him and sat down. "You know where we're going?" he said.

"Paris?"

"Yeah. After that."

"You know where it is. You've been writing to your pen friend. Or should've done. It's Canourels. In the Massif Central. Some fifty miles, I think, from the Mediterranean. We'll be in the mountains." She smiled. "I love mountains."

"It'll be totally uncivilised, won't it, then?"

"Yes. Wonderful."

"You some sort of wild girl, then?"

That would be a good image to have. "Could be," she said, then thought better of her reply. "Not really wild. You know, we've got to sit up all night, going through France, in the dark."

"We'll all be dead when we get there."

She laughed and gave him attention. He had a cheeky, freckled face and reddish hair that usually looked as if it never saw a comb. Today, though, his hair was smooth, his cheeks pink. What a shame it was about the slightly grubby hands and finger nails.

The party, about thirty Fourth Years in all, and two teachers, reached Paris and after a quick coach tour round the city, taking in Notre Dame, Sacre Coeur, the Eiffel Tower, La Madeleine, Paris Opera and the Moulin Rouge, they were taken to the Gare d'Austerlitz to board a the train that was high to climb into, to begin their overnight journey south.

The journey was long and boring. There was nothing to see through the carriage windows as it was dark. The seats were hard. This was the French third class carriage, not really for twelve hour journeys with a party of school children. Some grew restless, complaining a great deal, others tried to sleep. It was cold. Mattie was glad of her blanket, even if it wasn't as posh as Barbara's thick plaid rug. Conor snored. Mattie ached, but said nothing. Adventures were not adventures if you were comfortable.

The cold light of dawn revealed scrubland, mountains in the distance and rain. Houses or buildings of any sort were few and far between and unremarkable. Her visions of the south of France were soon abandoned.

At nine o'clock the next morning, the train at last pulled in to the tiny station of Canourels, a long, high platform in the middle of nowhere. Mist obscured mountains. It was so quiet, and even more so once the train had pulled out, leaving a party of English school children and their exhausted teachers, bewildered, yawning and disinterested in anything but sleep and perhaps, food and drink.

So, this was the Languedoc, foreign, rural, southern and isolated. Mattie was so tired, she saw little. She met her pen friend, Aline, older than herself, hair piled high, bosom hoisted high, skirt short, who took her to her home, which she also did not take in, where she slept for the next five hours in surroundings that were of no interest to her.

When she awoke, as if in a dream, Aline whisked her off to the church, where a funeral of someone notable in Canourels, was taking place. To Mattie's astonishment, she understood every word the priest said. She stood out in the churchyard where the coffin was lowered into the ground and four black-veiled daughters wailed, "Maman! Maman!" The church was old, with an orange roof. There were mountains all around, she could see now that the rain had ceased.

Tired and confused on her first day, Mattie spoke little, if any, French. She was alert enough, though, to be shocked by the toilet. Outside, through a scruffy backyard, behind an inadequate wooden door, it was nothing but a hole in the ground. She stared, shrugged, resigned herself. She'd get used to it, there was no alternative. This was an adventure. Get on with it. When she realised that she had to share the enormous *'bateau-lit'* with Aline, that was another shock. The apartement consisted of three rooms, two of them bedrooms, hers and Aline's leading from Madame's and Monsieur's and the children's bedroom. There was only one other room, a small kitchen which was a living room, also serving as kitchen and dining room. A large, long table, surrounded by chairs, was the only furniture.

In the dusty, grey Market Square the next morning, everyone met up, English and French pupils.

"The toilets!" was the main comment, despite the presence of the pen friends. Some English pupils reported bathrooms like they had at home. Others reported worse.

"My lot don't seem to have even a toilet," Barbara said quietly, staring at the cobbled ground.

"Where d'you go?" Mattie said.

"Outside. In the farmyard, apparently," Barbara said, turning her back and walking away.

Mattie laughed. "But, no, really…"

"That is really," Barbara said over her shoulder.

Mattie strolled over to join Conor on the other side of the square.

"Hi! How d'you get on?" he greeted her.

"Okay," Mattie said. "I live in that old castle-like place, on the first floor. That's their kitchen, that

171

window. There are two rooms off it, one of them, I sleep in, with Aline." She looked up at the ancient building. "That room, there, that window. That's our bedroom window."

"They nice people?"

"I don't know yet. They don't say much, nor do I. Lots of '*mercis*', on my part. You?"

"Okay," Conor said. "Like you, I haven't said much in French. You were right about the mountains. Look at them! What did you have for breakfast?"

"I had French bread, with white butter. I had to dip this into this malty-chocolate drink in a bowl. And then drink what was left, out of the bowl. It's lovely. You?"

"Coffee and croissant."

Drusilla and Barbara drifted away. Aline joined Mattie and Conor, whose pen friend, Gilbert, was giving a lot of attention to Angela Worthington, of 4G. Her pen friend, Claire, was looking across at Conor, who was totally unaware of this attention.

Aline, who was nearly two years older than Mattie, wanted to take her on a tour of Canourels. It was old, picturesque, set in a valley in the Central Massif mountains. A river ran to the south of the town, a wild, shallow, boulder-strewn mountain river. Mattie had her third shock since she'd arrived. There were women at the river bank, washing clothing, dashing garments vigorously against the stones and boulders. She stood still, watching them. Aline was saying something. Mattie could not understand so much French at once.

They met up with Conor and Gilbert, and a few others, when they returned to the square.

"A road goes along that valley," Conor said. "It goes by the river, through the mountains. Someone said we're going to be allowed to borrow bikes."

"I'll ask Aline," Mattie said. She turned to Aline. "*Aline, les velos?*"

Conor chortled. "I'd have been wrestling with my dictionary for ages," he said.

Aline responded with a wall of sentences in French, the last word of which was 'vendredi".

"Friday," Mattie told Conor. "I think they borrow them from their school friends, I'm not sure."

"A cycle ride along that road, that'd be super," he said.

Each morning, many of the pupils, English and French, congregated on the Market Square. It was a spontaneous action and, as someone observed, it seemed the sensible thing to do. Various activities and excursions were suggested. Groups or individuals would slope off, some to retire to a cafe all morning, others to explore. Bicycles appeared on Friday morning. Aline provided one for Mattie. Conor, she saw, had acquired one from Gilbert. Mattie abandoned a group who wanted to visit a convent out in the wilds, and went to meet Conor.

"I've seen enough convents in my lifetime," she told him. "We went to school at one, didn't we?"

"What d'you say to a cycle ride this morning?" he said as she approached him. "Looks like being a nice day, warm even."

"Who else is coming?" she said.

"I've only asked you so far. A lot of them are too scared to venture further away."

"I'll come. I don't see the point of coming all this way if I'm going to sit drinking coffee every morning. Once you've done that, you do something else, don't you?"

Conor stood grinning at her over his bicycle. "You seen Barbara Ellington this morning?"

"No, why?" It was a comfort to perceive that he didn't like Barbara any more than she did. She moved with Conor a short distance from the main group, wheeling her bicycle.

"She's got the letter-box mouth since she got here. She's grizzling every time I see her."

"She doesn't like it here, does she? She's staying out in the wilds."

"Reckons she's homesick this morning."

"I knew she was unhappy because they don't have a toilet, not at all, where she's staying. Just out in the field."

"No?"Conor chortled. "Is that right, now?"

"She told us. Her Mummy can't sort her out now, can she?" Mattie knew this was being catty, but she was talking to a boy and it didn't feel that wrong.

"Big baby." Conor dismissed Barbara for a more interesting topic. "Have you learned any swear words? It's the first thing most of us asked about."

"The ones I know sound rude, without even knowing what they mean. Aline taught me some in patois. I think it's the Languedoc language, you know?"

Aline joined them, wheeling a bicycle and Gilbert came over when he saw where Conor was.

"Aline," Mattie addressed her pen friend. "*Je voudrais aller avec Conor, au velo, ce matin. Que voulez vous faire? Non, pardon-moi, ce n'est pas correct.* Tutoyer! She's asked me to call her 'tu', the familiar. *Aline, ou vas-tu ce matin?*"

"Crikey," Conor said, under his breath, "you are taking it seriously, aren't you?"

Aline responded to Mattie with a tidal wave of

174

French this time. Mattie turned to Conor. "I'm not sure, but I think she wants to come with us. She's asking Gilbert. They most likely want to keep an eye on the bikes."

"Tell her we're off."

"Aline," Mattie said turning to the other girl, "*nous allerons.*"

"Crikey. Future tense as well," Conor said admiringly. Mattie smiled to herself and they set off.

Every morning, the host families provided lunch, a French stick of bread and garlicky sausage, for each of their guests and to their own offspring, often with a bottle of water or diluted red wine. Mattie balanced her own lunch bag on the handlebars of her borrowed bicycle.

The sides of the valley rose above the road and river, trees crowded above them. The ride was exhilarating. If Rosemary had come, they would have both have been too nervous to do anything like this. Conor was supporting Mattie's adventurous streak. In his company she could allow herself to feel bold.

"Remember to ride on the right," she yelled to Conor, who was ahead of her. The valley road was quiet, traffic was slight. Most of the time there was a silence that Mattie might have experienced as disturbing had it not been for Conor's robust approach.

After some distance, he dismounted and waited for her to catch up.

"Manourgue, eight kilometres," he said, indicating a road sign. "I don't know what that is in miles."

"I'm no good at maths," she said reaching him with a squeal of brakes. "About five miles?"

"No good at maths," he grinned. "Let's have a

break. We've got all day." She looked around them. There was a bank of grass and shingle beside the river. Conor laid his bicycle down on this. "I want a really good look around, instead of whizzing past everything."

"We can sit down here, we can paddle." Mattie rested her bicycle on the ground beside his.

"It'll be icy cold," he said. "It's only April even though it feels like July. The water has had to come down from the mountains."

"They're not mountains with sharp peaks, are they? It's more like one great mass of high land. I think it's a huge plateau." They sat on the grass and listened to the burbling river, strange bird calls and a whispering breeze. The sound of young voices reached them from the road as Aline, Gilbert and some others flew past.

"*Les autres*" Mattie said.

"The French kids," Conor said. "They didn't see us."

"I'm hungry," Mattie said. "I'm going to eat some of my picnic."

They sat on the bank of the river, on some small boulders, to eat their *petit dejeuner*.

"An awful lot of bread, isn't it?" he said.

"But it's lovely. I'm enjoying the whole thing, aren't you, the whole experience? I'm so glad I came. It's much more interesting and exciting than I thought it would be."

"I should think we both smell of garlic by now."

"Have you had frogs' legs yet? I have. Crispy and meaty but not very substantial. I've eaten moorhen, too. That's what it translated as in my French dictionary. All sorts of duck and fish, as well. Things unnamed. Madame keeps a stock-pot on an-old-fashioned range in the kitchen. For soup. The range keeps the kitchen warm. It's very small, I expect it's cold here in winter."

"The wine's good," he said and Mattie had to laugh. Had her conversation been too domestic?

"Good? Miss Dixon said that what we're drinking at meals is rough wine. It tastes it, too, rough on your tongue. I have two glasses every night. It sends me to sleep. Monsieur traipses down to the cellar every evening to fill a bottle from a barrel. It's all so – you know, so primitive."

"Life in the raw," and again Mattie was slightly amused at this schoolboy trying to be manly.

"Where I am, there's one tap, on the landing. I was surprised. When we were in the old house, we had one tap in the scullery and I thought that was shameful. But at least we had a proper toilet."

"Where d'you live now?" Conor's teeth tugged on the bread.

"Hill Common. It's a new house." How faraway it all was, unreal almost.

Conor put away the uneaten portion of his bread. He stripped off his jumper, spread it on the ground and lay back on it, stretching out, with his hands behind his head. Mattie did the same with Delia's ghastly flower-covered cardigan, not caring about mud or debris on it.

"This is the life," Conor sighed. "Forget mod cons and that."

Mattie gazed up at the bluest sky she had ever seen, against which stood out white rocks and green foliage. The steep sides of the valley rose behind them and across the river.

"It's bliss," she said. "Mountains. I love mountains."

"Funny, isn't it?" Conor said after a long silence, "how coming abroad makes a difference."

Mattie gave this comment serious attention. She had had similar sentiments but needed him to elaborate, in order to check that he was talking about the same kind of reaction as she had been experiencing.

"What d'you mean, funny? The difference to what?"

"Strange. Unexpected. A difference to how I see my life back home from here. Things get you down, don't they?"

"Why, do things get *you* down?"

"Yeah. Coming all this way, you get things in perspective."

"The world's a big place, isn't it?"

"My problems looks small, from here."

Mattie wanted to know more. "Do you have problems at home then?"

"Do I have problems at home! I'm glad to get away."

"Is it a big problem?"

"Yeah." He hesitated lifted his head to give her a quick glance and then laid back and shut his eyes again. "Me Da's an alcoholic."

Mattie took a deep breath. "Poor you."

"Don't tell anyone."

"I won't. Does it cause trouble?"

"Rows. No money. And it's scary. When it's real bad, it's scary, I don't mind telling you. Don't tell anyone, will you?" His voice was flat.

"I won't. How do you manage, with school and that?"

"It's my way out, my escape, my reason for living, except there's a lot of snobs there. I love me science. I focus on me work. I think about the future, a good future, my own future. I keep out of me Da's way." He glanced over to her again. "I've never told anyone this."

She raised herself up on one elbow and turned to look at him. He had his eyes closed, against the sun, against the facts, and against her to whom he had told his dire secret. The cheeky schoolboy was no more. She saw him differently, in a new light. The humour, the cheekiness, they were covers for a serious young person who knew trouble, who fought it, who had developed strategies for dealing with it and who had aims for getting away from it.

She scrambled to a sitting position on Delia's cardigan. "I'm going to tell you a secret of mine. I have kept it to myself for nearly four years, well, three years, really, because I didn't understand what was happening for the first year or so."

Conor remained perfectly still, eyes closed. "Go on," he said.

"My older sister had a baby. And she's not married."

"Crikey. I bet your parents made a to-do about that."

"My Mum did. Libby had to go away. Four years ago. Four years next month. She wasn't allowed to be in touch with me. I think Mum thought, and still thinks, she – you know – got rid of it. Or had it adopted. I don't know what she thinks. But Mum and Dad haven't seen Libby since, they don't know where she is. I do though. I go to see her, in London, every couple of months. And the baby."

"She kept it?"

"She did. And that's not all. The baby's father was black."

Conor's eyes opened . He sat up. "Crikey. Black. That's worse than being Irish, isn't it? 'No Irish, no coloureds, no dogs'."

"Mum wouldn't like it if she knew."

"I bet. Crikey, Mattie, you're strong, aren't you, keeping all that to yourself for so long and coming top in French all the time."

"Not all the time. My results last summer were bad."

"For you. You know, my work slips at bad times. But I'm damned if I'm going to let that toffee-nosed lot at the Grammar School know what goes on at home. They love a bit of scandal."

"I feel a bit like that, too. My Mum's ill. I won't use that as a reason for not doing well at school."

Conor turned a softer face to her, a face that had abandoned its usual bravado. "Any time you wanna talk, I'm yer man."

She giggled. "I'll do the same for you."

"You're a real friend." He said that to the sky.

Mattie went pink. "So are you."

"Good grief!" He jumped to his feet. "See that the bird up there?" He pointed to a large raptor circling overhead. "Bloody hell, it's a vulture. Quick. Let's go."

Rooted to the spot, Mattie watched the bird. Then she squealed, jumped to her feet, stumbling towards her bicycle. A lack of frenzy on Conor's part, made her turn to look at him. The familiar, cheeky Conor had returned. He was standing, shaking with silent laughter. She leapt towards him and pounded him with her fists

"Beast. You know it's not," she said, subsiding into laughter herself.

"No. There aren't any vultures in these parts. I think it's an eagle of some kind. Wonderful isn't it? Kind of majestic."

"I'm keen on birds as well," she said shyly.

"Are we going on to Manourgue?"

"Why not? We've come this far."

"Five miles, you reckoned."

"About that. I haven't ridden a bike for about five years. I'll hurt all over tomorrow."

"And no bath to soak in. Come on. Let's catch up with the French kids and teach them some more swear words, even invent ones that aren't real, just for fun."

"They're probably all in Manourgue now, eating ice cream and drinking lemonade."

"Or drinking coffee and smoking. I can't stand that horrid little Gaston. Let's pull his leg."

A peal of laughter escaped Mattie. Having unburdened herself, there was room in her for fun and Conor had a wealth of that on offer.

* * *

The three weeks Mattie spent on the French exchange visit to Canourels simply sped by. She decided that the arrangement of the universe that allowed this illusion was a cruel mistake. Gradually, more and more time was spent in Conor's company until, for the final coach outings to Gorges du Tarn and the caves on the Causse, they were together all their waking hours. Conor was a kindred spirit. He understood about having problems at home and not having much money.

While staying with Aline's family, there had been a letter for her from Libby, the first she had been able to receive from her without anxiety. She showed it to Conor. He might have wondered why she was doing so, but she wanted to share everything with him. Boys were different from girls, she concluded. Rosemary would probably have scrutinised it and asked questions.

On the homeward journey, passing in the train over

the Garabit Viaduct, one of Eiffel's lesser efforts, below the intriguing Le Puy, they arrived in Paris on a wet morning and Mattie's spirits were dampened. Back to Mum, back to her straight-jacketed life at home, good-bye freedom.

"I'm coming back one day, Canourels," she had vowed as she clambered up into the high train to Paris.

"Good-bye, Paris," she said tearfully at Gare du Nord. "Au revoir."

The train from Paris to Dieppe chugged through relatively uninspiring countryside in the rain. The Channel was rough. Delicate beings, like Barbara Ellington, emerged at Newhaven, white faced and damp haired.

Mattie, heeding Miss Dixon's warnings about customs, was concerned that she had more than her allowance of one litre of wine. Madame had given her half a bottle of rough red wine for the journey but also a bottle of good vintage as a gift for her parents. So Mattie tipped the remains of the rough stuff down the toilet on board the ferry and finding nowhere to leave the empty bottle, tucked it into her bag.

On the coach from Newhaven, she and Conor sat together in silence all the way back to Sittendon. At the Grammar School gates, crowds of parents and a number of cars waited.

"This is it," Conor said. Mattie's dampened spirits grew sodden. "Shall I see you in school?" he said, struggling to his feet.

"Of course," she said. She looked up to him. There was chaos around them. She could feel tears rising.

"Cheer up," he said and leaned down to plant a kiss on her cheek.

It was as though the world have been wiped of its misery. She smiled up at him. Swept up by the movement of anxious pupils in the gangway, he drifted towards the exit, glancing back at her with a cheeky grin.

She turned to the window to look for Mum and Dad. There was no sign of them. A brief glimpse and a wave from Conor, and he left with his case. No one had met him either. She collected her case from the boot of the coach and began to walk away.

"There you are!" a familiar voice said.

Mattie turned. It was Aunt Delia. "What are you doing here?" she said more in resentment than surprise.

"George is working and Rita is not well," Delia said.

"Mum's not well?" Again?

CHAPTER THIRTEEN

"So, is she bad?"

"Your Mum?" Aunt Delia lifted Mattie's case. "I think she's a bit better now."

"What's caused this?"

"Caused it?" Delia appeared to be playing for time. "I'd say worry."

Travel rug under her arm, Mattie hitched up on her shoulder the handle of the bag that contained the bottle of wine and the empty bottle. Delia, seeing that it was heavy, took a peek into the open top. "What's that?" she said

"What, the wine bottle?"

"Good grief, girl, you haven't drunk all that, have you?"

"No. Of course not. I tipped it down the toilet, because I was worried about customs." She could do without this aggravation from Delia. Coming home to wet weather, and leaving Conor, was hard enough.

"Oh, I don't believe that!" Delia put the case on the ground and stood, laughing a mirthless laugh.

"What are you trying to do? Show me up in front of my school friends? Come on, I want to find out how bad Mum is." Mattie walked ahead and Delia grasped the case to follow her.

When she reached home, Mum was sitting by the fire, a rug on her lap and the fire's doors wide open. Mattie put down her own rolled travel rug and the contentious bag.

"Mum, are you okay?"

"I am now. I was worried about you, in a foreign country."

Mattie kissed her. "Mum, you don't need to worry about me."

Delia followed her into the living room. "Rita, will you look at this?" She held up the empty wine bottle which she had pulled out of Mattie's bag. "Drunk as a lord. She must be."

"Oh, Mattie…" Mum began.

"No, I'm not." Mattie said crossly. "What d'you think you're doing, Delia, going into my bag? Stop it. All you want is a bit of excitement, isn't it?"

"Mattie, apologise this minute," Mum said.

Mattie couldn't bear it, so much antagonism so soon. She was having trouble being civil herself. "Me? Shouldn't Delia?"

"Delia, is it?" Delia said. "Who gave permission to drop the auntie?"

"Well, not someone who wants to think I drank that lot. I told you, it went down the toilet. I had more than my customs' allowance."

"Are you sure?" Mum said.

"Mum, do I tell you lies?" Yes, she did tell lies but only when forced to do so, not out of choice.

"How would I know?" Mum said. "I don't know you these days. You come back from abroad all cocky and full of yourself."

"Bloody hell! I wish I hadn't come back. I'm going to my room." She knew the bad language was over the top. She grabbed her bag and her case and struggled to get through the door.

"Will you listen to her, Rita?" Delia said. "She smells of garlic, too."

Mattie went upstairs. Mum did not seem to be too ill. Delia left after that. Mattie unpacked her case, sorted her laundry, later washing most of it. She prepared everything for going to her job at Phillips' on Saturday morning, two days later. The summer term was to start in the middle of next week and this year her birthday, her fifteenth, would be on a school day. She wrote a letter to Libby to explain that she would be unable to visit until the Whitsun half-term and that she had missed seeing her and Rosie over Easter. Mum had not been well again but seemed better now and there was not enough time before term began.

She was glad to escape to her waitress job on Saturday morning. Every table she wiped was done diligently, every customer's order she took was taken with a polite smile and total attention. The morning was altogether satisfying as much for the approval she received as the eight shillings she was paid at the end of the shift. When she reached home, going in by the back door, Mum was waiting for her, and waiting in one of her more formidable tempers.

"So!" Mum said as Mattie opened the back door. "You thought you were safely out of my reach, did you?"

Mattie froze. What now? "What d'you mean?"

"Boys! While you were in France."

Oh, no! Mattie was all ready to react in her usual defensive way but her new self had returned from France. She stilled her mind before saying, "Boys? How many?"

Mum was taken aback. She knew she was being mocked. That was good.

"One's been here. Looking for you. This morning."

"Didn't you tell him I was at work?"

"I did not."

To Mattie's surprise, this new approach made her want to laugh. Or was it because Conor had come to find her?

"That's a shame. But it doesn't matter. I know where he lives. I can go to his place."

"Wait!" Mum said as Mattie turned to leave again. "Where are you going?"

"I told you. To see him. At his home."

"Where's that?"

"Didn't you ask him?"

"I'm disgusted with you, seeing boys at your age."

"Not seeing boys, Mum. It's just one boy. A Catholic boy, the one who was at the primary school with me. I'm not doing anything wrong, nor anything I shouldn't."

"St. Angela's? You're encouraging this friendship. You don't know where it might end."

"Yes, friendship. That's exactly what it is."

"I want it stopped."

"I'm not stopping a friendship. What's the matter with you?"

"I'm worried about you. You'll get yourself into trouble."

"Don't judge me by your standards." And with that, she stepped back over the doorstep and pulled the door shut.

* * *

There it was, the house with the lop-sided garage, on the corner of Victoria Road. Stooping over an upturned bicycle, in front of the garage, was Conor. Mattie stopped walking to watch him. He was engrossed in his work on the bicycle. He must have sensed her eyes on him for he glanced up, his gaze going directly towards her.

"Hi!" he called, a big grin on his face. "I came round to your place this morning."

"I know." She strolled over to him. "Mum told me. I was at work."

"Yeah, she said." He reached for a grubby, oily towel on which to wipe his hands. "I forgot. You okay?"

Now, she was. "Yes. You?"

"Grand," he said.

They stood regarding each other, a barrier of shyness rising between them.

"I wish we were still there," she managed at last, taking two steps closer to him.

"I do, too," he said. His face was pink. Hers must be scarlet by now, but this was Conor, it didn't matter. He was self-conscious too.

"Have you –?" he began.

"I didn't –," she began at the same time.

There was an awkward pause before the tension was broken as they both started laughing.

"I was going to say have you got a bike?" he said.

She moved over to the flight of steps that led up to the front door of the house and sat on the fourth step. "I haven't. I was going to say I didn't know you had a bike of your own."

"Haven't ridden it for ages. Thought I ought to look at it. I was hoping we could go out on Monday if you'd agree to borrow my mum's bike. She'd be okay about it."

"That sounds…" She paused, not wanting to sound

too keen. She was more than keen. Why else had she postponed a visit to Libby on one of the last two days of the Easter holiday? "a good idea. Are you sure about your mum and her bike?"

"Certain," he said. "She hardly ever uses it now. I'll check it over before Monday. There's Tizer indoors. You want a glass?"

Her birthday was on the second day of the summer term. Much to Mum's annoyance, she invited Conor with Rosemary and Lola round to tea on the day, offering to pay for it out of her wages. Mum was less than agreeable to this, but nonetheless obliged to a minimal degree and only hovered discreetly when the friends were there. Mattie went to bed that evening feeling that she had won a quiet victory on the first day of her sixteenth year. The way to respond to Mum's negativity was to override it with as normal a cheerfulness as she could muster and pretend there was no problem.

Tony gained an interview for a place at the Grammar School. This was largely overlooked by the family. "It's getting to be boring," Frank said.

At Whitsun, during the week's holiday for half-term, Mattie went to visit Libby in Greenwich. Libby appeared to be remarkably well and happy, her demeanour, usually tinged with sadness, was different. She was upright and laughed a lot. Something had changed since Mattie had last seen her in February. Rosie was growing fast. She would be four in September. When she thought of Mum and Dad not knowing about her, Mattie grew sad.

"I've got a doll's house," Rosie said, leading Mattie by the hand to Libby's upstairs sitting-room.

"Show me, Rosie."

"It's a big one," Rosie said.

It was indeed a big doll's house, and well-furnished, too.

"You should have told me, Libby, and I could have bought some furniture for it. I'd have liked that."

Libby smiled. "It's only right that you spend your money on yourself. I'm glad you enjoyed France."

"I don't think the French kids' visit here will be so enjoyable. That's in just over a month. After the exams."

"What will they do, the French kids, because your term won't have ended, will it?"

"Outings will be organised for them. I wouldn't have minded going on some of them myself."

Mattie was on her knees, examining the miniature furniture of Rosie's doll's house. Rosie was busy watching her, and snatching the items from her if she thought her auntie was taking too many liberties and removing furniture far too long.

"That goes there," Rosie said. "No, not there. There!"

"It's lovely, isn't it?" Mattie wondered whether to confide in Libby about her friendship with Conor, but decided against it. "Where did you get it?"

"Feel," Rosie said. "Put it back. Put it there." She indicated where a little chair should go.

Mattie had examined the furniture. It was wood, beautifully made. "Feel?" she repeated.

"Feel," Rosie said, with emphasis. "Feel gave it to me. Feel."

"Who's Feel?" Mattie glanced up at Libby.

"Phil," Libby said. "A friend. Did I tell you, Auntie Grace has been unwell?"

"No, you didn't mention it. When was this?"

"Over Easter."

"When I was in France? You should have told me."

"You couldn't have done anything, certainly not from that distance. She is on the mend, now, anyhow. But she's getting old, Mattie. It's my duty to look after her. She looked after me."

After the Whitsun break, which was mostly spent in Conor's company, on Conor's mother's bicycle, it was exams. The atmosphere at home during this time was no more conducive to revision than the bicycle rides with Conor were.

"When are you going to return that bike to that woman?" Mum said more than once after having occasion to go out to the shed for deckchairs during a spell of hot weather.

"When I get my own bike, I suppose," Mattie said.

"I hope you're saving up for it because I haven't got any spare money for one."

"I'm saving up for other things."

"Like what?"

"We have been told that, in the Fifth Year, when we go back in September, that there will be opportunities to go on theatre trips and things during the autumn and winter."

"Theatre trips," Mum said. "I thought you were there to get educated, not to go gallivanting. I don't understand. All this business of going to France, then them coming here, disrupting the household, where's the sense in it?"

Mattie did not respond. She was preoccupied by another problem. Rosemary was jealous of the time she spent in Conor's company in school.

"You're always with him," she complained one hot lunch time. Mattie had met her outside the school canteen. It was lunch time and she had made her routine hasty return from home with a sandwich in her hand.

"No, I'm not. Not always."

"You used to be my friend. Now you don't have time for me. He's your boyfriend really, isn't he?"

Mattie said she supposed perhaps he was.

"Do you kiss him?" Rosemary's tone was petulant

"No. I've never kissed him. And I won't tell you if I do. It's personal."

"See? Keeping secrets from me. Real friends don't have secrets."

"He's kissed me," Mattie offered.

Rosemary stopped walking to regard her with a scowl. "Has he? See? How many times? What kind of kissing? Was it, you know, like on the films?"

"You are nosy, Rosemary. I'll tell you. It was just the once. On the cheek. As he got off the coach, here, outside school, when we came back from France."

"Was it nice?" Rosemary looked at her sideways.

"It made me feel weak all over, excited, exhilarated and at the same time, it was as though it hurt, here, when he went." She patted her chest, over her heart, "as though he was being torn away from me. It makes me sad to think about it."

Rosemary stared at her with a wide-eyed expression. "That's love," she whispered. "That's true love. I do envy you, Mattie."

At home, in her bedroom, Mattie wrote a poem about Conor.

192

When I see you,
It's like being given
Something that I want.
My heart smiles.

* * *

Mum and Dad received a letter to say that Tony had passed the Eleven-plus and would be able to start at the Grammar School in September.

Mum glowed. "I've scored a hat-trick," she told Delia.

"*You* have scored a hat-trick?" Mattie laughed. "Who do you think made all the effort?"

"Oh my, she really is full of herself, isn't she, Rita?" Delia said.

The French kids arrived. Bribing her brothers had ensured that there was no acrimony concerning the use of their bedroom by Mattie and Aline during the three weeks of the visit. Tony, who received the biggest bribe, half of Mattie's Saturday morning wages for one week, slept on a camp bed in Mattie's little room, while Frank had her bed. There were outings to London for the visitors and their hosts to see the sights. Mattie spent much of the time in Conor's company, even when with Aline, compensation, she told herself for her poor exam results. Her parents did not say it, but she knew they thought the friendship with Conor was the cause of those poor results. So did her teachers. After the French visitors had returned to France, she and Conor were free to spend the rest of the holidays together, except on Saturday mornings, when she worked at Phillips' and the odd extra days which she was offered during the holidays of regular staff. She was unable to visit Libby until just before the beginning of term in September. This would be the visit for Rosie's birthday. Efficient searching had produced some exquisite little dolls for the doll's house. She bought two of them and with pride, wrapped them to take on the journey to Greenwich.

Libby seemed to be going from strength to strength. Rosie demonstrated her less charming side.

"For the doll's house?" she said, having unwrapped the proudly presented gift. "I don't play with my doll's house now. I've got a doll's pram. I want bigger dolls now."

"Rosie, that was unkind," Libby said. "Say you're sorry."

"Sorry," Rosie said, without looking at Mattie. "Look, this is my dolls pram. Phil gave it to me."

Upstaged by Phil! Well, whoever this Phil was, she had a lot of money to spend on spoiled Rosie.

"Why?" Mattie said.

"For my birthday," Rosie said. "Phil's kind."

"Who is this Phil?" Mattie burst out, turning to Libby. "Who is she?"

Rosie was right there, close to Mattie. With all the contempt she could muster she said, "Phil is not a lady. He's a man."

Mattie's heart gave a big jolt then seemed to stop. All sorts of reactions fought inside her to come to the surface. The first was rage, unreasonable but so strong. How dare Libby do this, after all the care and concern she had expended on her sister? Libby had come first for a long while, keeping her secrets, lying to Mum, the journeys to see her. How dare she? And to be secretive about it.

194

Now Mattie was embarrassed. She knew she was jealous. She wanted to be the most important person in her sister's life. Even Rosie was a bit of a nuisance in that respect, though she was only little and easily dismissed. Mattie turned hostile eyes to a retreating Libby.

"Why didn't you tell me?"

"I thought I'd wait until I knew which way it was going."

"And which way is it going?"

"Serious," Libby said.

Mattie fought with herself to keep the tears back. Her eyes and her throat ached with the effort.

"I'm sorry, Mattie."

"You're not sorry. You look thoroughly pleased with yourself. I've been wondering why you looked so well."

"If you stay longer this time, you can meet him."

"Meet him? I don't want to meet him." The time, the effort, the secrecy, the anxiety – was it all to hand Libby over to some unknown man who would come first in her life, and Rosie's, for ever and ever? Mattie wanted to scream.

"I would like to think you're happy for me, Mattie. I have been so lonely."

"I want to go home," Mattie said.

She said goodbye to Auntie Grace who, down in the sitting room, now a bed- sitting room, seemed more frail since she last visited. Then she slammed out of the front door. At last she could let go and give in to her tears. But she was unable to do that. They had been held back so forcefully, she could not let them go.

She caught the next train to Sittendon. She stared, unseeing, out of the window, her eyes aching as though they were made of glass. From Sittendon station, she marched straight to Victoria Road, where Conor lived. He was there, in the shabby living room, watching television. His mother showed her in. He jumped up.

"Mattie, what's happened? Are you upset about something?"

"Come for a walk with me. I'll tell you. Let's go down by the river."

She set the pace, an angry, fierce march. There was an autumnal feel in the air, as though summer was tired and it was time to retreat towards the darker days of winter and a life in which Libby was not so important. She sat on a bench and patted the space beside her.

"I went to see my sister. I found out, after all the things I've done for her and Rosie, that she's got a boyfriend." Mattie burst into tears.

She felt his hand creeping into hers. Her sobs subsided. He gave her hand a squeeze.

"So what?" he said. "So have you." He leaned closer and gave her a peck on the cheek.

She sat still for a moment, then she moved closer to him, flung her arms round his neck and gave him a light, soft kiss on the lips. Sad and angry feelings flew to be replaced by emotions and sensations so sublime she didn't know what to do other than to bury her face on his shoulder. She was aware of his arms folding around her. Life was suddenly perfect.

FIFTH FORM
1954

CHAPTER FOURTEEN

"You are now in the Fifth Year," Taffy Jones Two, the new form teacher for 5S, told them on the first day of the Autumn term. "This will be a year of hard work, hard application, leading to grand results in your O-levels next summer." He then went on to list some of the less gruelling prospects of life in the Fifth Year.

"'Romeo and Juliet' at the Old Vic in September," he said. "In October, an orchestral concert at the Royal Festival Hall, to include a symphony of Beethoven's, and Sadler's Wells Theatre in November to see Puccini's '*La Boheme*'. I'll be collecting money for seats and coach fares the week after next. Please be prompt with the correct amount for the trip in which you wish to participate."

Mattie, bothered by her worst exam results ever, at the end of last term, sought a quiet word with Mr Jones in the moments before the bell went for assembly.

"I don't know if I'll be able to get all the money by then," she said, "I was thinking of giving up my Saturday job, but these trips are important to me. My results at the end of last term were not so good. I didn't know about these outings."

"They are part of your education, really. Would your parents find it difficult with the money?"

She nodded, biting her lip.

"Well, if you do give up your little job, there can be help. You won't be the only one. Let me know, will you?"

"Do I need to do anything else?"

"Beyond getting a parental consent form signed by your parents to give permission for these trips, no."

Mattie made a face. Diplomatic relations between the generations had never been so poor in the Dobson household. Frank was being challenging, finding the Third year changes a shock. He was in a science form. Tony seemed not to be waiting to settle down at the Grammar School before confronting parents and teachers alike. Mattie looked away. If there was a problem obtaining a signature she knew only one way round it. And that way was wrong.

"Have you thought of giving up the boy-friend?" Mr Jones said.

She gave him a scornful glance. "Why would I do that? He helps me with my science homework." Taffy Jones Two taught science, specifically physics. By the Fifth Year she was less easily intimidated by her teachers.

"I'd like to see you do well in science," he said, "you and Flynn."

She decided not to give up the Saturday job. As she predicted, Mum was reluctant to sign the form giving permission for her to go on the trips.

"I don't see the sense in it, late nights and that," Mum said. "What about getting up in the morning? You've never been good at that at the best of times."

"Okay. I'll ask Dad."

Dad, however, never betrayed his wife. "If Mum won't sign it, it's no use asking me to do it behind her back."

She asked Mum again. She would not even deign to reply to Mattie's request.

Mattie was becoming desperate. She was also determined and far calmer than when she was younger, in the face of this sort of lack of understanding.

"Don't worry, Mum. If you won't sign it, I won't go to school." With that she returned to her room, took off her school uniform, put on her night clothes and wriggled down under her eiderdown, with the intention of sitting, or rather lying, it out. Let Mum explain her absence to the teachers at the Grammar School.

Unexpected support came from Tony. "I'll do the same," he said, "because I want to go to a football match on Saturday." He was as rebellious as his word.

By eleven o'clock, Mum gave in. Mattie returned to school to give Mr Jones the form, duly signed, with the required money, and Tony went back thinking he was going to the football match in London on Saturday. Mattie was obliged to support Mum when she told him, on Saturday morning, that he wasn't going, she had no money for such jaunts. Mattie hid his shoes and was late to work, the first and only time.

* * *

Mattie had no best coat to wear for the trips, only her short, shabby school raincoat. She didn't care. There were more important issues to occupy her mind. On every trip to London she sat next to Conor. There was a certain glory about that. She didn't need smart clothes to boost her confidence. Rosemary, because of the impossibility of getting home afterwards, chose not to go. Lola was not interested.

'Romeo and Juliet' at the Old Vic was a revelation. Dry words on a page, obscure ways of saying things, played out before her, became vividly alive to tell a harrowing story. Beethoven's Pastoral Symphony at the Royal Festival Hall sent her spirits soaring. The depth of feeling rising in her as she watched 'La Boheme' at Sadler's Wells left her crying all the way through the fourth act and half way home.

"I never understood 'the arts' and all that and what it meant," she said to Conor beside her on the coach. "I couldn't see it all as anything more than a posh sort of entertainment, theatres and so on. It's much more than that."

"What is it, then?" Conor said.

"The arts? They show you life. They show you emotions, experiences. They tell you about people and relationships. They tell you about yourself."

"That's made psychologists redundant, then?"

"Of course. Live music! It's wonderful."

After the coach left its youthful passengers at the gates of the Grammar School, she ran the short distance home. Mum and Dad were in bed. She remembered to lock and bolt the back gate and the back door as she went in.

"It was wonderful," she called bounding up the stairs to her bedroom.

"Hush!" came Mum's equally loud voice. "Don't wake the boys."

Always the squashing comment, the silencing. What could she do with her exuberance, then, but lie in bed and relive the performance. At school the next morning, she spoke to Taffy Jones Two in the corridor. She had to tell someone.

"The opera, last night, it was incredible. I'm so enjoying these trips."

"I'm glad you are getting a lot out of them, Martha."

"I'm thinking things, like about my life."

"I hope you're thinking of staying on to Sixth Form. There'll be more like this. It's not all nose to the grindstone, you know," he told her.

"I might stay on," she said.

At lunch time, she dashed home to make herself a bacon sandwich.

"It's not good for you," Mum said, "all this dashing about."

"Probably not." Mattie washed her used utensils under the tepid water from the hot tap. Hot water cost money. "Who cares when life is good!"

"You'll learn to care," Mum said. "I see you're still wound up from last night."

"Yeah. It was wonderful. You should do some of these things. You'd be less grumpy if you did."

"What with? Shirt buttons? I've never had the chances you three have had."

Mattie watched her, the lined face, the dead eyes, the permanent frown. She was sorry for her, a futile sorrow. There was nothing she could do to help her. If there was, Mum would resist somehow because in a way, she was comfortable in her misery. There was a stubborn pride there, too. Her life would end like Mimi's in 'La Boheme' all sad and unfulfilled, wasted. With this dramatic interpretation of her mother's life, she hurried out of the house as the boys came in for their lunch. She went back to school in a state of happy melancholy.

The day was bitterly cold. Conor emerged from the school canteen having made his meal last as long as possible in order to stay out of the sharp wind. He shrugged himself into his gabardine raincoat as soon as he saw Mattie.

203

"Can we walk round for a few minutes?" she said. "I need to talk."

He shoved his hands deep into his pockets and hunched himself into the scarf wound round his neck. "Make it brief," he said.

"It's about my life."

"Your life?" He glanced up at her from his scarf cocoon.

"Yes. I'm seeing it differently. I'm thinking of staying on to the sixth form."

He smiled above the scarf. "I'm glad. That's what I want to do. Why the decision now?"

"After last night."

"Mimi dying, you mean?"

"No, not that. Not Mimi at all. This whole thing, opera, music, theatre. Can I come round to you on Saturday? Straight from work? To talk?"

"Sure."

"I'd say come to my place, but I don't want Mum to overhear. I had thought I ought to go to London to see my sister, but she's changed. She doesn't need me now she has a man in her life." At that moment, she could have become teary. To her relief, the bell shrilled throughout the school and over the deserted playing fields to announce the beginning of afternoon school.

* * *

Mattie set off for work at Philips' on Saturday. A scone or a sandwich was allowed at the break half way through the morning, so this time she chose a sandwich to be an early lunch. The weather was still cold. The store was busy, Christmas being close. This year, she could not engage with the preparations. Life had been easy over the summer with warm weather, light evenings, so seeing Conor had been no problem. In December, unless they had money to meet in a coffee bar for frothy coffee, there was nowhere to talk about the serious side of life. Growing up seemed to mean that the serious side of life was becoming most of it. It was sad, in a way.

Conor's mother had a roaring fire in their living room. She stayed in her kitchen, baking. Mattie greeted her there and was offered a slice of bread pudding.

"I've been thinking," Mattie said to Conor as she sank onto the settee and her teeth sank into the bread pudding.

"That must be difficult," Conor said.

"Oh, funny. When I first started at the Grammar School, I had no idea what it was all about," she said. "I thought education was sitting, listening to what clever adults knew. But that's changed."

"I've always loved science. Especially physics," Conor said.

"That's my least favourite of everything, except for algebra. Listen. These outings to London, to concerts and the theatre-- I see now. I don't quite know how it happened, the understanding. I did so enjoy the opera."

"I did too," Conor said.

"It was everything-- music, drama, colour, dance. I want to see more. There are going to be visits to art galleries next term. That's education, too. It's why we go. There's more than knowing facts. There's understanding other things. I'm not explaining myself very well, am I?"

"Yes, you are."

She rose, going over to the fire where she stood with her back to it, turning a glowing face to Conor. "It's about appreciation. Beautiful things, sad things. The trip to France. That was part of it. Appreciation…" She paused. He was laughing, possibly at her. "I don't know how to explain. Don't laugh!"

He gave a great chortle to which she responded by launching herself at him. They both laughed, pretending to fight. Suddenly, it all stopped. She was half-lying over him. His expression changed at the same time as her amusement vanished, replaced by something else, something mind-stopping.

"You're a smasher," he said, from his position half-beneath her.

She caught her breath, aware of the feel of his body so close to hers. He was warm, strong, alive. She dropped her head to his chest to inhale the scent of him. His heartbeats were audible. A powerful magic seized her. Her heart smiled.

It was too much. She straightened up, pushing her hair from her face. "I'm learning to appreciate…" Her voice faded. She wanted to say "the opposite sex," but that was too outspoken. Anyway she was a bit shy – no, very shy.

The moment passed. They both sat up and rearranged themselves to sit meekly side-by-side. "You've got to stay on," he said. "Next year. We both can. You're clever at English and French."

"I'd really like to."

"I plan to go to university, to have a career, the whole thing."

"Will your parents agree?"

"No problem. Yours?"

"I doubt it. Especially my Mum. My parents have got three of us at the Grammar School. It's difficult for them. Money, you know."

"Have you asked them?"

"I don't dare."

He grinned. "I dare you," he said, "the two of us, in the sixth form, together, I like it."

She could feel the smile creeping over her face. Her enthusiasm was re-ignited by his eagerness. She liked it. She loved the prospect. She loved Conor. That must not be put into words, despite the compulsion to tell him. That was the route to the same fate as Libby's, and probably no Sixth Form, which would be a disaster because she knew now, with no doubt at all, even without Conor, that was what she wanted – to stay on for two more years and do her A-levels.

"I dare you," he said again. "You know you ought to."

"I will. After Christmas."

"Do it now."

A loud voice out on the street distracted the attention of both of them.

"Me Da," Conor said, with a groan, all liveliness fleeing his face.

"He's only singing," she said, "sort of."

"Right now. Been drinking all day. At his mate's."

The 'sort of' singing voice moved to the back of the house, banging and crashing ensued. Mattie heard Mrs Flynn's voice, a protesting squeak.

"Come on," Conor said, "get your coat."

"Where are we going?"

"To the church."

"At this time? It's dark."

"Just come with me. Please."

Conor snatched his own gabardine raincoat from a hook in the hall, grasped her hand, to lead her out of the front door and down the steps to Victoria Road.

"We'll sit in the church," he panted as they half-ran. "Me Mam will join me later." "Stay with me," he said.

She felt a rush of sympathy for him. She had had no idea he had put up with such scenes.

"Of course," she said. There was nothing that would make her relinquish his grasp on her hand.

"One of these days," he muttered, "I'll sort him out. For the time being, though, this gives me Mam peace of mind. She can deal with him and not have to worry about me."

"How long will you stay in the church?"

"Until Father Tully turns us out. Me Mam says it's the only good turn he's ever done us, letting us stay a while."

They reached the church. Inside it was gloomy but warm. Conor settled on a pew at the back. Mattie recalled the time she had used the place as a refuge herself. The red light of the Sanctuary lamp, blinking its comfort, brought the memory back. She mooched around, lighting candles she couldn't pay for, and saying prayers she had a cheek even to think up. Mrs Flynn appeared after half-an-hour with what Mattie suspected was a black eye. In the gloom, she could not be sure.

Later, Conor walked home with her. She went indoors the back way, chiding herself for being a coward. She would raise the subject of the Sixth Form. She had nothing like the problems Conor was dealing with.

Mum and Dad were watching television, the boys

sitting obediently on the settee. Mum glanced at the clock as if she was about to say, "What time do you think this is?" Since it was just after seven o'clock, she couldn't because it was too early for complaint.

"Do you want some tea?" she said. "It's out there, in the kitchen, waiting."

"Actually, I want to talk," Mattie said. Her heart was thumping.

"Come on then," Mum said, her attention still attracted by the television screen. "Sit down."

Neither of the boys showed willingness to make room for Mattie on the settee so she perched on the arm.

"I can't talk really, not with the TV on." The temptation to say, "Turn that row off," had to be resisted.

"What about? What do you want to talk about?"

"Mum, I want to talk about my future."

This alerted Dad. "Oh! Yes. I was talking to Bob Granger only this week. You know, the one whose daughter works at the bank?" He leaned forward to switch off the television set, drawing groans from Frank and Tony.

"Can I have your scone?" Frank asked Mattie.

She shrugged. "If you want to." She was still aware of Mrs Flynn's bread pudding nestling weightily in her stomach

The boys went. Dad, all keen, wanted to talk about Bob Granger's daughter who worked at the bank.

"Dad, I don't want to work at the bank."

"It's a good career," Dad went on.

Mattie slipped down onto the settee. "No, Dad. Listen, I want to do other things."

"For a girl like you," Dad persisted, "it would be ideal."

"Only until you get married," Mum said. "You want to get married, don't you? Otherwise, why do you hang around that Conor lad so much? All girls want to get married. And have children."

"Yes, I want to do that. Eventually. Not necessarily with Conor, though." Mattie's voice was calm, but inside, she was anything but calm. Thoughts were boiling in her mind, her mouth was dry and her level of anxiety was rising by the second. "I want to do other things first."

"Like what?" Mum said. Her tone was abrupt now. Her anxiety was rising too.

"Like, well, actually, staying onto the Sixth Form –."

"Mattie, this is nonsense." Mum would not look at her. "We live on a council estate. Your Dad works for Parks and Gardens. That sort of thing is not for the likes of us. If we lived on Gracehill, like Veronica Fitzgerald –."

"Veronica couldn't get into a Grammar School. I did. I want to stay on to the Sixth –."

"To do what?" Dad said. "You might just as well leave and go to work in the bank. What good will the Sixth Form do you?"

Mattie jumped to her feet. "You don't understand. In the Sixth Form, you do A-levels. If they're good enough, I can go to university." There, she'd said it, she had dared to say it.

The effect on her parents was stunning. Mum looked at Dad, Dad looked at Mum. The silence was unnerving.

"This is nonsense, Mattie," Mum said, her voice icy.

"We are ordinary people," Dad said.

"We don't send our children to places like that," Mum said.

"You've done well to get to the Grammar School. Now you can use that to get a good job at the bank," Dad said.

"I don't want to work at a bank. I want to study French and go to university and get a degree. In London, if I can, because there are theatres and concert halls there."

"Oh, a life of gallivanting, is it?" Mum was angry. "Going to France, the theatre, getting up to all sorts of things. You will not be doing any of that. What would Father Tully say?"

"Amen, I expect." Mattie tried humour.

"Oh, you and your Grammar School skit. The sooner you leave the better. As for staying there longer than you need--"

"We can't afford it," Dad said, interrupting Mum as if he had found the final good reason.

"You can get grants!" Mattie's voice was becoming louder. She was desperate. "You can get grants. I've told you."

"Don't talk nonsense," Mum said.

Dad was on his feet now. He stood to confront Mattie, which was unfortunate for him, not realising that she had grown taller than both her parents.

"You can stop this nonsense right now, Mattie," he said. "We can't have you looking down on us."

No! He couldn't have said that! Mattie was breathless. Her Dad, her quiet, gentle, reasonable Dad, coming out with such a statement , looking and sounding ludicrous and so desperate, so fearful that he could not really have understood the implication of what he was saying.

Mattie burst into tears.

"You can stop that," Mum said. "Crying won't get you your own way."

"This has been the problem ever since I went to the Grammar School, hasn't it?" Mattie heaved and sobbed. "You're afraid I might look down on you. What disgusting nonsense is that? You should be ashamed even to think that."

"You'll do as you're told and leave school and go and work in the bank."

That was Dad? She couldn't believe it, his true colours at last and she didn't like them. Her sobs grew louder. "I wish I'd never been born!" she screamed, rushing from the room.

From her bedroom, she could hear her parents talking, their voices carrying more than usual. She sat on her bed. Her wages from this morning were still in her pocket. What a long time ago that was, her shift at the coffee shop, an eternity. So much had happened, so much had changed. Conor would be allowed to stay on to the Sixth Form. She had felt sorry for him, she thought his problem huge compared with hers. Not any more. Her problem was enormous, it was her life. Of course, she could try the trick of refusing to go to school on Monday morning. There were two drawbacks to that–Sunday to be lived through first and anyway, at this stage, it would be a triumph for her parents. They would be relieved if she didn't go to school. It would be a small sign of hope for their point of view. It was going to school that was the problem.

CHAPTER FIFTEEN

After a while, she was calmer. She bathed her tear-swollen face in cold water and sat a while longer. The money in her pocket was demanding her attention. She came to the decision.

Creeping downstairs was not difficult. Her parents were still preoccupied. The boys were in the living room, trying to watch television. A lot of noise came from there. She grabbed her coat and scarf and made a stealthy exit through the back door and the back gate. Still adjusting her clothes, she almost ran down the path to the pavement and round the corner. The curtains at the front downstairs window did not twitch.

She trudged her way across the town in an icy wind. At the railway station, she purchased a single ticket to Victoria. Until her problem was solved, there was no way she would return home. Not many people were travelling in this direction at eight o'clock in the evening. Her steely resolve wavered on the journey until she remembered her work was better this term. The teachers said so. What a waste that extra effort would have been if she did what her parents wanted her to do.

She hurried past the ticket barrier at Victoria to the bus stop to catch the trolley-bus to Greenwich. London at night was not attractive, even so close to Christmas, because of the ghastly sodium lights. Everyone looked ill in the orange glow.

At Greenwich she alighted. She all but ran to Libby's

house. She rang the door bell. No one answered for what seemed to be a long while although Libby must be at home because there was a light on at the upstairs window. Presently, she heard footsteps, bolts being withdrawn and a key turned. The lights were switched on illuminating the stained-glass panels in the door. The door was pulled back cautiously to reveal Libby's face peering round it.

"Mattie!" she gasped. "What are you doing here at this hour? Did you get my letter?"

Mattie became hysterical. She flung herself at Libby, clinging to her with a fierce grip. Libby staggered backwards, closing the door, holding on to her, to sit on the stairs where Mattie could be supported in more comfort.

"What is it, Mattie? What happened? Is it Mum? Dad?"

"Yes. No. I don't know."

"Are you in trouble?"

"Yes. No. I don't know."

After what seemed an age she quietened, her body becoming limp. Her head ached, her throat hurt, she was dizzy. "S-sorry. S-sorry," she said.

Libby rocked her gently as far she was able to, squashed on the staircase.

"What do you think might have happened?" It was a new voice, a man's voice. Someone else was here. The realisation shocked Mattie. She opened swollen eyes and peered through the banisters at the side of the stairs. A man stood there.

"Hell!" she said, angry. "Who are you?"

"This is Phil," Libby said, all chirpy.

"That's all I need," Mattie said and closed her eyes again.

Libby and Phil laughed soft laughs.

"Can we get you upstairs?" Libby said. She was trying to extricate herself from Mattie's grip. "Then you can tell me all about it."

Libby sat her in a chair and gave her a glass of water, which she took from Phil. He hovered. Mattie shot him a glance of intense dislike.

"Did you get my letter?" Libby said again.

"What letter?"

"I sent to it your friend, Lola. Did she not give it to you?"

"No. When?"

"About two weeks ago."

"No. She was off school for a couple of days. I remember. What did it say?"

"About Auntie Grace. She died. Over a month ago. I wrote to tell you once the funeral was over. I haven't seen you for ages, not since, when was it, September? October? I don't see so much of you now."

"I didn't know. About Auntie Grace. I'm in the Fifth Year now. It's a lot of pressure. What are you going to do? Where are you going to live?"

"It's all fine. No problems. Just tell me why you're here and what's been happening to you?"

So, between sips of water, Mattie told her.

"Who is Conor?" was Libby's first question.

"A boy in my form." Mattie gazed around her. There was no sign of Rosie and Phil was not in the room now. "Where's Rosie?"

"Asleep. It's late."

"Who is Phil?"

"He's Auntie Grace's sister's son."

"Dad's sister too? Doesn't that make him your cousin?"

215

"No. There's a lot you don't know, Mattie. Phil is making some tea and some sandwiches for you. I don't expect you've had much to eat, have you?"

"Bread pudding, at Conor's, about two o'clock this afternoon." Such a long time ago. Mattie felt weary thinking about it.

The door creaked open slowly and Phil appeared, bearing a tray of the promised tea and sandwiches. He set it down on a small table near to Mattie, who eyed it hungrily.

"You tuck in," Libby said, "and I'll explain. Phil, you stay. There are no secrets, are there, Mattie?"

"None of mine," Mattie said, giving Phil a meaningful glance.

Libby sat close to Mattie. Phil lounged alone on the settee.

"Phil is Auntie Grace's sister's son. Here comes the difficult bit. He is not related to me at all, neither was Auntie Grace, bless her." Libby paused.

Tired, Mattie could not understand all this. Concentration was an effort. "What d'you mean?"

"That's because Dad," Libby said this slowly, "is not my father. Careful!"

Mattie's cup and saucer moved violently as she gasped. "What d'you mean?"

"I was born two months after Mum and Dad married."

"Are you adopted? Is Mum your mother?" She put the cup and saucer on the table and moved herself forward, reaching her hand out to Libby. "Oh, bloody heck, Libby, the hypocrite. The way she treated you."

"No, no! You must look at it another way. I don't know the whole story, what happened or why. In those

216

days, it was all hushed up and Auntie Grace didn't know much, only what I'm telling you. She did tell me what a lovely man Dad is, marrying Mum, bringing me up and passing me off as his own."

"He's not lovely. Dad betrayed me. He let me down. I really thought he'd stand up for me, Libby, I really did."

"Well, of course he didn't stand up for you. He stood up for Mum. He supports Mum through thick and thin. This is just another example, your argument today with them."

"And you've done the same thing as Mum, haven't you?"

"She's so disappointed in me. Can you see that's what made her so angry with me?"

"I suppose so." Mattie had to agree but it was done grudgingly. "She's angry with everyone, you know. Does Delia know?"

"I imagine so. He was Irish, my father. They'd all rushed over from Ireland, to hide it. Grandma, Mum and Delia. Then Mum met Dad. Auntie Grace said he was a saint."

"This is all too complicated for me." Mattie yawned. "Don't make me go home. Not tonight."

Phil sprang up from the settee to hurry from the room.

"There's another one," Libby said softly.

"Another what?"

"Saint." Libby laughed. "You'll like him when you get to know him."

"Will I?" Mattie wanted neither to get to know him nor to like him.

"He's a teacher at that big new school in south London a comprehensive school."

Had Mattie been a puppy–and she felt as soppy, as floppy and as innocent as one–her ears would have pricked up. Her sudden flicker of interest exhausted her and she yawned. "What does he teach?"

"Maths and physics."

"No! Really? My two worst subjects. Conor loves physics. He helps me with my homework. Lola was helping me with algebra but I think she's got a new boyfriend. She used to go out with Barry next door. That's why she forgot the letter, I expect." From the little that Lola had told Mattie, she was probably 'up to No Good', as Mum would have put it.

The door opened and Phil edged his way in. In his arms he held a huge pile of bedclothes which he dropped onto the settee.

"You can sleep on the settee tonight," Libby said.

Mattie watched Phil make up a bed for her. He must be a kind man, to do that. He smiled at her when he saw her watching.

"Thanks, Phil," she said but to please Libby, really. "What's a comprehensive school?"

"All abilities. No eleven plus."

"No snobs?" Mattie yawned again. She realised how tired she was.

"Talk and plans tomorrow," Libby said.

If she had not been so exhausted, Mattie would have resisted the possibilities suggested by those words. A while later, in one of Libby's glamorous nighties, she crawled into her made up bed on the settee. As she drifted into sleep, she could hear Libby and Phil in the next room, talking in subdued tones. They couldn't possibly be sleeping together, not after all that had happened, could they?

Rosie woke Mattie the next morning.

"Wake up, Mattie. Wake up. I got a biscuit for you."

Mattie woke up. Rosie was standing close to her, a plate in her hand bearing a biscuit. She gave every appearance of not wanting Mattie to take it. Libby stood behind her, offering a cup of tea.

"Oh, luxury," Mattie said. "You can have the biscuit, Rosie."

Rosie snatched the biscuit and abandoned the plate.

"The plan is this," Libby began.

Mattie's stomach turned over in a wave of fear. "I don't want to go home."

"We're all going down to Sittendon, in Phil's car. We'll see Mum and Dad. She's going to have a terrible shock. Don't forget, she thinks, at the moment, that she's lost her two daughters and she'll be blaming herself. She'll say things she doesn't mean."

"M'm," Mattie said, thinking maybe Phil would sort everything out. He was a teacher and he had a car. They would listen to him, Mum and Dad. When she saw the possibilities, the relief was so enormous, she would have agreed to anything.

They set off early from Greenwich, Mattie sitting with Rosie in the back seat having to listen to and respond to, without complaint, her niece's endless, tireless chatter.

As they approached Sittendon, the upheaval returned to Mattie's insides. Libby leaned over the back of her seat, flapping her hand in an odd way.

"By the way, I forgot to tell you. I put it all in the letter that you never received. Phil and I are married. It

219

was a very quiet register office ceremony, not long before Auntie Grace died. She was so thrilled, she changed her will. The house belongs to both of us, sometime after Christmas." She pointed to the ring on her left hand.

"Gosh!" Mattie said.

"Just thought I'd give you a little yarn to ponder on. Oh, and I'm taking A-level English and maths in June. How about that! I hope to go to university."

"Oh, you crafty thing!" That would persuade Mum and Dad too.

The scene as they approached sixty-four Oakfield Road was alarming. A group stood around the front door, every member of which stared as Phil's car drew up at the kerb. Phil got out first. Mum, with Dad beside her, was on the doorstep. The boys were there, looking bemused. Mattie spotted Conor, and his mother. It was a black eye.

Mattie could see it clearly from the pavement. There was Mrs Wood, from next door, on the path.

"I'll be the advance party," Phil said. He and Libby strode hand in hand up the path. Mattie, trembling a little, followed, holding onto Rosie's hand. A low sun glinted on the scene. It was cold but bright.

Nobody on the doorstep moved until, without warning, Mum pushed everyone aside, stumbled from the doorstep, her voice cracking and hoarse as she tried to say, "Libby." Arms wide, with convulsive sobs, she threw herself at her.

Mattie cried, Libby cried. Rosie, agitated, detached her hand from Mattie's and clung to Libby's skirt. Conor appeared next to Mattie, to take her hand.

"I dared," she whispered to him.

"Like hell you did," he said and gave his cheeky grin.

"Come in, come in," Mum was saying after what must have been ages. "It's cold out here, come in, everyone."

Mum and Dad, Libby, Rosie and Phil, crowded into the living room, Dad promising to light the fire. Lola disappeared after explaining that Mum had tried to contact everyone she knew was Mattie's friend. "Your Mum has your letter," Lola said. "I forgot. Sorry."

Mrs Wood ushered everyone else into the kitchen-diner, saying she was going to make tea and did Mattie think, "the wee coloured girl would like some milk?" Mrs Flynn went home but Conor stayed.

Presently, Mum came out to the gathering in the kitchen-diner.

"Mattie," she said. Her voice was different. She sounded open and less hard. Mattie pushed her chair back and shaking went round the table towards her. Mum held out her arms. "I'm sorry, Mattie," she said. "Really sorry."

Mattie responded and hugged her. Mum felt different, soft and lovely, like a Mum should. Like she used to feel.

"You must have your future, Mattie," Mum murmured in her ear. "You must have the future you want. Dad is in agreement, too."

THE END

Acknowledgements

Thanks to Matt Maguire, of Candescent Press

to Pete Currie, Laura Probert and Sylvia Daly, and

to all my friends for their support and
encouragement.

Also by Maggie Redding

ALMOST PARADISE
A humorous novel about the older generation in
which the funny characters are the younger ones and
the real people are the ones with wisdom and
experience

HOLD FAST TO DREAMS
A story about a mother of four daughters who leave
London for an idyllic life on the Welsh Border, which
turns out to be less than idyllic.......

A LIFE WORTH LOVING
A teacher learns about life

COMMON GROUND
A family moves from one end of the town to the
other, where life is very different.

Available from AMAZON,
on Kindle or in Paperback

If you would like to be put on my mailing list or to
contact me
you can do so by viewing my website and blog at:-
www.maggieredding.com

Printed in Great Britain
by Amazon